GWENT

FOLK TALES

GWENT

FOLK TALES

CHRISTINE ANNE WATKINS

For the Gwent motherline
… and the fatherline, too.

First published 2019

The History Press
The Mill, Brimscombe Port
Stroud, Gloucestershire, GL5 2QG
www.thehistorypress.co.uk

British Library Cataloguing in Publication Data.
A catalogue record for this book is available from the British Library.

ISBN 978 0 7509 8679 3

Typesetting and origination by The History Press
Printed and bound in Great Britain by TJ Books Ltd

CONTENTS

Acknowledgements

My joyful thanks go to the many people who have helped me research the stories in this book. First and foremost, to all the tellers, noters, mutterers and shouter-outers of the tales and fragments of tales. I'm glad I heard what they had to say.

To the work of Fred Hando, whose wonderful books and sketches of the 'shy corners' of the Gwent landscape were eagerly bought and passed between my gran and her sisters in the 1950s. Battered and irreplaceable, the books live on my shelves now; I often consult them and always find them inspiring.

To the people and organisations who are walking their talk, actively researching the land of Gwent and its histories. To the hugely knowledgeable Frank Olding for several things, from an iron-mountain walk to the foreword for this book. To Evelyn Jenkins for her excellent research on wells, especially Gwladys' Well, and to the Twmbarlwm Society for boots-on-the-ground sheer hard work.

To the staff at Gwent Wildlife Trust, Newport Wetlands Nature Reserve, Pontypool Museum, Gwent Archives, the National Library of Wales and Monmouth Museum. To Richard Urbanski for help along the way.

Huge thanks to staff at The History Press and to Cath Little for making the link; and last but by no means least the heroic illustrators who have helped bring the pages to life: Katherine Soutar for the marvellous cover, Stuart Evans (pp. 17, 39, 51, 65, 69, 73, 77, 87, 111, 117, 125, 131, 135, 147, 155), David England (pp. 29, 35, 83, 103, 107, 123, 167, 170), Lily Constance Urbanska (pp. 13, 43, 57, 91) and Janusz Llywelyn Urbanski (pp. 23, 95, 161).

Diolch o galon.

FOREWORD

The honoured place of the *cyfarwydd*, the storyteller, in Welsh society is as old as Wales herself. In the fourth Branch of the epic medieval saga of the *Mabinogi*, Gwydion, the great warrior–magician, comes to the court of Pryderi, the hero of the Four Branches:

> They entered, disguised as poets. They were made welcome. Gwydion was seated next to Pryderi that night.
>
> 'Well,' said Pryderi, 'we would like to have a story from some of the young men over there.'
>
> 'Our custom, lord,' said Gwydion, 'is that on the first night we come to a great man, the chief poet performs. I would be happy to tell a story.'
>
> Gwydion was the best storyteller in the world. And that night he entertained the court with amusing anecdotes and stories, until he was admired by everyone in the court …

The old tradition still thrives in some corners of Wales and these folktales of Gwent reach far back to those ancient ways and customs. Christine Watkins stands firmly in that honoured lineage; she has taken up the mantle of Gwydion and the ancient storytellers who won the admiration of prince and pauper alike for their 'amusing anecdotes and stories'.

In Gwent, in our small corner of Wales, the old stories have other resonances. These old folktales have survived persistent and determined attempts over the centuries to suppress the language and Welsh identity of our county. Thankfully, those attempts did not succeed but generations of the children of Gwent were deprived of their heritage and their birthright. In preserving and re-telling these tales for a new audience, Christine has righted an old wrong. Let her be 'admired by everyone in the court'!

Frank Olding
2019

INTRODUCTION

I spent the first part of my childhood in the village of New Inn, in the Eastern Valley of Monmouthshire, where many generations of my motherline and some of my fatherline had lived. Some had come from their fields and their trades to mine ironstone and coal, some were here long before, farming the land.

In the house built by my great-grandparents I could look out every morning through the front room window and see the Rising Sun – not the heavenly body, but the pub of the same name. In the back of the house, from the bedroom window of the room where I was born, I could see Mynydd Twyn-glas, and Mynydd Maen resting her shoulder. My mother told me that, if I woke in the night, rather than calling her I should just go over to the window and look out at the mountain, with its lighted 'mast', and I would know that all was well. Old Stone Mother, the mountain herself, never slept, even if flesh and blood ones did. Her dark skirts are threaded through with whinberry roots. Her blood flows iron, and through her body run shining seams of coal and long, deep caves, where sharks once swam and left their teeth embedded in her bones. She is wise and watchful. And sometimes she may make herself known to you, just a little. And when she does, it is by no means always a comfortable thing.

Some of the stories you will find here come from fragments my grandmothers tucked into their skirt waistbands, gathered with twists of wool as they walked the hill paths. Or, in later years, slipped under their hats as they selected a cream cake from the cake stand and drank their tea on a rare day off in town. Others have been carefully saved by different folk.

In researching this book I've done a lot of walking, remembering and some forgetting, too. When pathways disappear from view, you have to find a new route, a way round, or strike out in some other direction. I have needed to discover quite a few new routes through some of the stories in this book. Sometimes, when it has been the only way I could find to tell the tale, I have taken some of them in a new direction. I've tried to include stories from across the old county of Monmouthshire, the 'pleasant land of Gwent', from the mountains to the sea.

Looking down towards my home village from the mountaintop, you will see Llandegfedd Reservoir just a little further beyond. The reservoir was created in the early 1960s. Following a public inquiry, the farms and houses were acquired by compulsory purchase order and the water was pumped into the valley from the River Usk, since the only natural stream there is the little Sôr brook. For generations, my foremothers and fathers had walked the footpaths through the valley going about their daily business, visiting family, sharing news. Now their paths stop dead at the lake edge, reappearing on the far side. I'd need to be able hold my breath for a long time to walk their routes again.

The daffodils that my gran picked every year with her friends in the fields at Pettingale Farm now bloom and sway beneath the waves. If I look hard enough from the top of the mountain, I glimpse them.

Christine Anne Watkins
2019

1

HEN WEN

She was certainly old. Her eyes were tiny and deep and they twinkled with something like ancient starlight journeying out through the cosmos. She knew all the paths over land and over water; she had crossed continents and gone rootling far and wide beneath the trees, poking her snout into the earth. And long ago she had dived down into the depths of the sea to rest and there she had stayed for

many, many generations. Hen Wen, the Great Mother Sow, Old
and Blessed, her name hidden deep in the oldest stories, herself
hidden deep in the sea. Far beneath the waves time rolled on and
at last a precious burden began growing in the womb of Hen Wen.
And the time came when she felt the pangs of birth coming on,
and she swam up from the deep to find a birthing ground. Yes,
she came rootling, rummaging and grunting from deepest story,
making her way to the muddy shoreline of Gwent Is Coed, with
her burden of abundance and fertility. She approached from the
south-east, and there was someone with her; a swineherd who had
been on the lookout – and now he had her in his sights. The swineherd's name was Coll, son of Collfrewy, and he had his work cut
out for him, because really there was no herding this old sow. So he
was trotting along beside her as best he could, making sure to keep
his hand in contact with her bristly flesh at all times so as not lose
track of her. He was determined to stick with it.

On came Hen Wen, until she reached Aust Cliff at the edge
of the great river estuary. And when she reached the clifftop, she
stood for a moment or so with her snout into the wind. There was
the grey-blue sky; there was the grey-brown expanse of water, and
there on the other side was Gwent Is Coed – Gwent below the
wood, and the wood itself, stretching away into the distance. After
spending a few moments savouring the breeze, Hen Wen trotted
on. Quite straightforwardly she went, stepping out into thin air,
right over the edge of the cliff. And Coll, who knew that he had to
keep his hand on her whatever it took, he went over too. For that
alone you could have said that he earned his place in song as one
of the Three Powerful Swineherds of the Isle of Britain. But that
wasn't all. Down she plummeted, Hen Wen, a pig in space, serene
in the fine fresh air for a couple of seconds until she entered the
Severn Sea with the most enormous splash, setting off her own
little tidal bore. And down went Coll too, since at that point he
had no choice.

Once she was in the river, Hen Wen became hippo-like, revel-
ling in the cool water, which was very soothing for her birth pangs.
For a while she drifted and swayed and then she dived down deep.

Slowly, ponderously, rolling her body this way and that, Hen Wen let the powerful currents carry her further out into the flow. And though the river is wide and the currents are fierce, they were no obstacle at all to Hen Wen. Coll held on and kicked his legs mightily. He held his breath in the murky greyness until he felt that his lungs were near to bursting. Then at last Hen Wen rose to the surface, right in the middle of the river, and floated for a while, looking around her with mild interest, blowing and breathing. Coll just about had long enough to take a couple of lung-wrenching gasps of air, then down went Hen Wen again, letting her pains, which were really quite monumental by now, be soothed and eased by the tides.

At last she beached, in the mud where the gulls were feasting by Aber Tarogi, at the place called Porth Is Coed – Portskewett. Not sure if he was dead or alive and still grimly clinging on to a handful of bristle, Coll lay for a moment blinking up at the sky, retching and spewing up water. But on went Hen Wen, hauling up through the squelching mud and Coll staggered to his feet and went slipping and slithering after her. She made her way unhesitatingly up from the water and around the edge of the great forest, the remains of which we now call Wentwood. She did not go in under the trees, but skirted around to the foot of Mynydd Llwyd and there she stopped and lay down. And her sides began to heave as a labour of vast proportions got under way; Hen Wen, old and blessed, farrowing abundance. Coll's sides were heaving too, because he still hadn't got his breath back and he was still full of river.

And Hen Wen grunted and rolled and squelched and then at last she squeezed out … a grain of wheat. Yes, one single little grain. It lay there on the damp mud, golden, complete. Within it golden fields stretched wide to the horizon, a whole land of plenty. And Hen Wen's sides continued to heave until she birthed a second time, and this time out came a tiny little bee, complete and furry. And the newborn bee rested for a moment beside the grain of wheat, drying its wings in the sunshine. Coll knelt to watch it, his breath growing calmer and his gasps slowly dwindling into a few hiccups. As he watched for a moment it seemed to him that he saw a paradise of stalks grow up and wave golden, and wide meadows full of flowers bending with the weight of bees, and the air shining with pollen. And from that day the place where the grain and the bee were birthed has been called Maes Gwenith, the Wheatfield.

Hen Wen lay quiet for a while, tired from birthing such a generous landscape. The little grain of wheat was already burrowing down, burying itself in the rich ground. The little bee, as soon as its wings were dry, set its course, rose up into the air and went buzzing away. Hen Wen heaved herself to her feet. As she did so, Coll was sure he glimpsed the imprints of stalks of wheat on the sow's hide, ears of corn marked out across her flesh and red clover and woundwort and knapweed. Hen Wen paused and looked at the swineherd for a moment, her little eyes twinkling from the depths. Then she turned her snout northwards along the coast and trotted on her way. Once again, Coll stretched out his arm and grasped her bristles, and kept pace by her side. They say Hen Wen never stopped till she reached Pembrokeshire, and then only long enough to birth another bee and a grain of barley. They say that in the North she bore fiercer fruits – she even bore a kitten who grew into a cat bold enough to challenge Arthur himself. It was a hard enough journey for the swineherd Coll, son of Collfrewy, but he stuck with it. And in Gwent Is Coed wheatfields waved abundant and golden as far as the eye could see, there was good bread to fill the belly of all those who hungered, and the air was heavy with the scent of wildflowers.

2

THE STAR-BROWED OX

An ox came walking steadily through the mud, out of the autumn mists. It was and was not an ox like any other. It was huge, it was white. It had a black mark shaped like a star high on its forehead. It came moving on, brushing past brambles and branches and nothing slowed it down at all. The mud was deep and gluey and splashed up where it walked, but the feet and legs and flanks of the ox remained white as could be. Because this was and was not an ox like any other.

The ox walked on into a dream. Yes, it just pushed the gossamer walls of the dream aside and shouldered its way in and stood there for a few moments. This dream was not just any dream, but one that was being dreamed by Gwynllyw, ruler of the land that lay between the River Rumney and the River Usk, the land bounded by the coastal plain to the south and the wooded hills to the north. Gwynllyw's land was good land, with its seashores and plains and lofty wooded groves, but Gwynllyw had gone to sleep that night, and for many nights before, with one question on his mind. 'Where oh where,' wondered Gwynllyw, 'in all my good lands can I build a dwelling?' He had a dwelling already, of course, but he desperately wanted another one, a new and special one.

And as he had done for many nights already, he lay awake in the small hours wondering and fretting about this question. He could build pretty much anywhere he liked, really. Nobody was going to stand in the way of Gwynllyw; he had might and right on his side, he was a fighter, feared and admired on land and on sea. He could build anywhere he chose – but that was the problem because, try as he might, he had not been able to decide on a place. And he had started to think that it was almost as if he didn't know how to decide, and that thought irked Gwynllyw, because if there was one thing he had always prided himself on, it was being decisive. He had decided he would have Gwladys for his wife the minute he laid eyes on her. And he'd got her – even though it hadn't been straightforward and her father King Brychan Brycheiniog had taken some persuading. And the famous Arthur and his men had ambushed them and would have taken her from him if they could have. Yet that time was long past and now Gwynllyw almost seemed to have forgotten how to make choices: he was frozen by indecision, and he found it to be a strange and horrible feeling.

So really it was quite a wonderful thing that as Gwynllyw lay tossing and turning that night, half awake and half asleep, an angel had actually come and explained to Gwynllyw where he should build. Or rather, he had explained how Gwynllyw could discover the place. The angel had begun rather generally, talking about a riverbank and a little hill, and then he had gone on to describe how

Gwynllyw would see a white ox there. He was just describing the ox in more detail – white, a black star below its horns, signalling all good things to those whose path it crossed – when the ox itself pushed its way into the dream and stood looking around with mild interest. At that point the angel's descriptions became a bit redundant, because Gwynllyw could see quite well for himself. Still, the angel shuffled a few discreet steps to one side to avoid being barged into by the ox and stoutly persevered with the message. The land on which Gwynllyw found the ox, said the angel, would become his and he would cultivate it with the ox's help. And as the angel drifted away, these words echoed on after him:

There is no retreat in the world such as you will find in this place which you are destined now to inhabit. Happy therefore is the place, and happier therefore is he who inhabits it.

Gwynllyw woke with those words still sounding in his mind. He remembered his dream very vividly. He fought hard to keep the details in the forefront of his thoughts, not let them fade away. He felt a surge of certainty and it was very welcome. It was clear to Gwynllyw now that he didn't actually have to *choose a place*, he just had to *choose to follow* – unconditionally. And that is what he did the moment he opened his eyes. His retinue were dumbstruck when Gwynllyw announced then and there that he'd had a dream and that he was going to build a sacred dwelling in a place that would be indicated to him. He concluded the brief announcement by adding that he was handing over the running of his lands to his son, Cadoc, with immediate effect. Having made his decision known, Gwynllyw did not for an instant pause to doubt or reconsider. He strode off and began to wait and keep watch in likely places, by rivers next to hills. Throughout the months that followed, Gwynllyw never wavered in his determination. He had found the decisive feeling again and he liked it.

It was snowing lightly when Gwynllyw saw the ox. Without hesitation he began to follow and he continued to follow until at last they came to rest. There on wild land where no furrow had been cut, there on Stow Hill, Gwynllyw rolled up his sleeves and began the work of wattle and daub, raising his house. A house sacred to the glory of creation. When Gwynllyw's son, Cadoc, saw his father toiling in the snow, raising the house of his dreams, he sighed – and even though he was very busy with all the new duties that had been handed over to him, he took time to come over and nod knowingly. Cadoc was a saintly individual with a tendency to say wise and noble things even when people hadn't actually asked for his opinion. 'Ah!' said Cadoc. 'Not to those who begin good things has glory been promised, but to those who persevere!'

Gwynllyw, who had been persevering for quite some time already, just smiled and continued and when Cadoc had gone away Gwynllyw whispered to himself:

There is no retreat in the world such as you will find in this place which I am destined now to inhabit. Happy therefore is the place, happier then is he who inhabits it.

And even when the snow turned to blizzard, Gwynllyw did not pause in his labours. For if the air was freezing, he, Gwynllyw, was unfrozen, and the way had opened before him at last.

Now all this time Gwladys, wife of Gwynllyw and mother to his children, observed the work of her husband. She said little, though she knew many things. She knew the ox paths; she trod them in her dreams. But Cadoc had words of wisdom to impart to his mother, too. When he began to speak to her concerning the importance of living a goodly life, not ruled by fleshly matters, Glwadys responded by setting up her own house of prayer a furlong or so away, and for a while that seemed to keep Cadoc at bay. She and Gwynllyw still bathed together in the River Ebbw, as often in the dead of winter as in summer, if not more often. Then they would return chilled to the bone, and did not easily heat up again but lay, four cold legs in a bed. But Cadoc still felt the need to continue advising them both on matters of flesh and abstinence. The upshot was that Gwladys moved another five furlongs away. She didn't see much of Gwynllyw then, though occasionally she thought about Arthur and the ambush and days long past. But mostly Gwladys swam alone in the river; floated in a rare slow pool in the fast-flowing Ebbw, and her thoughts were of strawberries, hay and wild dog roses. The hay she used to dry her feet when she came up out of the river, the roses and the strawberries she took to the Lady's altar and placed them there as an offering. When she returned to the river, she said:

There is no retreat in the world such as in this place which I am destined now to inhabit ...

For the rest of her days she swam there, strong-boned and sturdy, like an ox at the plough. And whenever Gwladys dreamed, in her dreams it was summer.

When the sacred dwelling of Gwynllyw was complete, it was his final resting place. The deeds of Gwynllyw were felt to be great and strange and were spoken of long after his death. One of the best poets of the land began a great work in praise of Gwynllyw's life. Unfortunately, he experienced writer's block and keen though he was on his subject matter, he sat for the best part of a year trying and failing to write something that would speak about the glory of Gwynllyw, and his sacred dwelling on the hill. Writer's block is a cruel thing, really; it dams inspiration not quite at the source, but very soon after. The poet sat and struggled all through the winter, which that year was particularly hard. If Cadoc had been on hand to deliver his words of wisdom about perseverance, the poet would probably have punched him.

But it must have been his destiny to write this work, because when he had been struggling for a year and a day and was lying on his back wrapped in a blanket feeling as if he would never be warm again, a high spring tide came flooding up the river, carrying all in its path. People ran, but the water was faster, and carried them away before they could reach the safety of higher ground. People and animals flailed and sank beneath the waves, houses were washed away, but as it turned out the house where the poet was holed up was one of a small number that were *not* washed away. Instead, as the waters began to rise and rush, the dam had held the poet's inspiration in check burst – and then and there the great poem of wonder at the life of Gwynllyw began to flow from him. He started to write at the table, but as the waters rose he climbed a ladder and continued balanced on a rafter. He perched there for three whole days while his house was filled with waves, and when the waters finally receded the countryside all around was a muddy morgue. But the poet and his house had survived; spared, he supposed, precisely in order to write of the strange deeds and dreams of Gwynllyw.

3

THE WATERS SALT
AND SWEET (1)

When I was a little girl in the 1960s I often travelled by rail on
family holidays to visit my great aunts, who had decamped from
Monmouthshire to live amongst the palm trees of South Devon.
One of the first adventures on the journey began when the light
disappeared with a whoosh, a dark world filled the window and
my ears went quiet inside. The Severn Tunnel. And always the
question not to think about ... *what if the sea comes pouring in on
our heads?*

This is a question that must have been confronted by the engineers who planned the tunnel, of course. It probably wasn't ever very far from the minds of the hundreds of men who went down and did the actual spadework either. But as it turned out, it wasn't so much the salt sea channel above them that the tunnel builders had to worry about. It was the sweet, winding waters deep in the earth that had long been running in their own secret and particular way.

In the coastal marshlands of Monmouthshire, large springs of bright clear water bubble up to the surface in several places. The rock strata that form the hills of Wentwood a little to the north – limestone at first, then old red sandstone – are cracked and broken beyond their base, and the water that runs down from them has found cunning subterranean channels. These channels gather and flow into the valley of the little Nedern brook as it passes on its way to the Severn. Now, it was known that the Nedern, rising as a small stream in the hills above Llanfair Discoed, would sometimes suddenly run dry, losing all of its water near the foot of the hills, only to burst out again just as suddenly at a place near Caerwent called 'The Whirly Holes'. For longer than anyone could remember people had told tales about the Whirly Holes – but surely those were just little tales told to warn children not to play too near the water? Surely they couldn't be of much relevance to the great endeavour of the tunnel-builders?

In October 1879 the building of the tunnel had already been under way for six years and was making good headway. In fact, there was only about 500 feet left to go between the shafts they had driven down to make the first 'headings' on the Monmouthshire side and the Gloucestershire side. Then all of a sudden, somewhere between Sudbrook Camp and Portskewett, all the water that had flowed so long from the hills, finding its own little pathways through the rock, gathered itself up and began pouring into the tunnel. The Great Spring had arrived, and in style. The Great Spring was not a quiet stream, it was not a gentle trickle; it flowed into the tunnel at a rate of 360,000 gallons an hour, causing almost every well and spring for miles around to run dry. There were three pumps on the Monmouthshire side but these were quickly overwhelmed as the tunnel flooded. The only reason no lives were lost was because the men in the heading were actually changing shift when the waters broke in and were able to escape through one of the shafts.

All work in the tunnel was stopped. For the next few years every effort was focused on trying to outwit the Great Spring and the sheer power and volume of its waters. Firstly, of course, it had to be stopped from keeping on rushing into the tunnel. Two heavy oak shields were made, shaped to cover the two entrances to the top headings, then lowered down an old shaft and wedged tightly into position by oak beams, then sealed with tar. This seemed to work. The next step was then to get the water that was already in the headings out again. So new pumps were ordered and heaved into place. They worked, then they failed. Then they worked again, and then they failed again. And each time they failed back leapt the Great Spring, flooding the tunnel. And each time the tunnel flooded, rails and bricks and upturned carriages full of waste rubble would be tumbled here and there and left lying like drift-wood. And each time that happened, divers were sent down into the chaotic darkness to investigate.

The divers' suits were cumbersome and their equipment was heavy and the pressure at depth was very hard to bear. Worst of all, they had to drag their long air hoses behind them, making sure they didn't snag on the piles of debris they had to clamber over. The chief diver on the team was a man named Alexander Lambert. Again and again he went down into the pitch dark-ness and the cold, to fix problems with pumps, locate leaks, adjust seals and valves. In particular there was a heavy sluice-gate that they needed to close but found they could not. All in all, it looked like it had come down to a contest – the world's bright-est engineering team and three thousand-strong workforce versus the little Nedern brook and its gathered waters. And the Nedern brook was winning.

Then something happened; one of those strange synchronicities that probably made the difference between the tunnel getting built or being written-off as a heroic failure. What happened was that the lead engineer, Thomas Walker, who was getting desperate by now, heard about a marvellous dress. This marvellous dress was such a new thing that hardly anybody knew about it yet, but the very thought of it must have made Thomas Walker lift up his head and hope. Mr Henry Fleuss's Diving Dress worked by means of its own breathing bag connected by a length of copper tube to a rubber mask. This new device would, if Mr Henry Fleuss's calculations were correct, allow the wearer to work under water for a couple of hours at least completely independent of a cumbersome air hose. But as yet this was all still largely in the realm of speculation because Mr Fleuss had only just invented the Diving Dress and he hadn't even had time to test it in a working environment. In fact, it had hardly been tested at all, other than on an eighteen-feet dive off the Isle of Wight whilst tethered to a rowing boat. But Thomas Walker said to himself, 'Cometh the hour, cometh the man,' and sent for Fleuss, who duly arrived to take a look at what all this tunnel flooding business was about.

It took Thomas Walker a long while, despite his powers of persuasion, to get Henry Fleuss to agree to go down into the chaotic darkness of the flooded tunnel and test out his new invention; but he did. Fleuss set off into the tunnel, putting his life on the line, walking the track in his marvellous dress. Though really it wasn't so much walking as crawling. Fleuss had to labour on his hands and knees in the deep mud between the rails, inching his way forward in the blackness. Under such conditions, Fleuss's nerve failed before the Diving Dress could prove its worth and he came back out from the tunnel, swearing that nothing would persuade him to go back into those hellish conditions.

But it was enough to convince Thomas Walker that the new diving apparatus could help save the day. He decided on the spot that lead diver Alexander Lambert should be called for and sent down to continue the trial that Henry Fleuss had been unable to complete. On a November afternoon in 1880, Lambert accepted the instruction from his boss and began his journey into the black tunnel. With Walker, Fleuss and a small circle of onlookers waiting anxiously above ground, Lambert walked and scrambled for an hour and a half until he reached the door, where he lifted one of the steel rails and turned one of the valves as required. However, perhaps more than a little nervous about the new equipment he was using, and with no way of knowing how long he had spent underwater, the job of lifting the second rail defeated him and he returned to the surface with the job still not complete.

But now the apparatus really had proved its worth and Lambert was keen to complete the job. A couple of days later he set out again, and in an eighty-minute dive he retraced his route to the door, removed the second rail, shut the door and turned the second valve as instructed. Unfortunately, he turned it the wrong way; it was later found to be left-hand threaded. But even with this setback, within a couple of months the water level was low enough for foreman Joseph Talbot to open the door in the shield and see if it was safe enough for the engineers to come in. It was. And on the next day, nattily dressed in the soon-to-be-redundant old-style divers' suits, with sou'westers instead of helmets, the party of engineers waded through water up to their waists to view the debris that was piled up at the point where the Great Spring had broken in. They decided to build a brick headwall eight feet thick with an oak door set in it to stop the Great Spring while the building of the tunnel continued.

With the brickwork set and the oak door in place, the Great Spring was duly sealed off in early January 1881, temporarily controlled but not yet beaten. It was still there, just on the other side, contained behind brickwork and other fixtures, and its pent-up pressure on the rock strata all around was intense. So, in due course a permanent pumping station was built that was capable of pumping out twenty-five million gallons of Great Spring water per day. Today, the pumps in the pumping station are electrically driven – but they're still at work, pumping the same quantities of sweet, sweet water every single day from the Great Spring.

4

THE WATERS SALT
AND SWEET (2)

Afon Hafren, the Severn river, is the longest in Britain and wound deep into the history of this land. Like the Wye, which forms the eastern border of the historic county of Monmouthshire, it rises in Pumlumon's marshy ground, where many waters bubble up. The Severn doesn't meet the Wye again until it is fast becoming an estuary – the Severn Sea, as the Bristol Channel was called until Tudor times, and still is in Welsh – Môr Hafren. The two waters meet and mingle at a place called The Treacle, near the little island of Chapel Rock. As river opens into estuary and into sea, so its stories open into one another; they are washed and smoothed by waves, buried in mud and changed from their original shape – and some of them concern Habren, the goddess of the river.

There was a time when Locrinus was King of England. Locrinus was descended from Trojans, and he was a fighter. He fought off invasions in the North, from bands of Germanic warriors and on one occasion he pursued their great leader, Humber, into the river, where he was drowned and which afterwards bore his name …

Now, Locrinus was a fighter but not, by nature, a vindictive one. He tended to take prisoners when possible. And amongst the prisoners taken at the time of the battle with Humber was a woman named Estrildis, who was a high-born member of the invading Germanic tribe.

And casting his eyes over the prisoners as they stood lined up awaiting their fate, Locrinus noticed Estrildis. And as soon as he had set eyes on this captive, he himself was captured. It may be that Estrildis saw in that one swift glance that Locrinus was as much a lover as he was a fighter, and she seized on that as her one chance for freedom. Or it may even be that she raised her eyes to his and that thing happened, that thing that we call love at first sight. But however it was, that one quick glance was followed by one longer gaze – and Locrinus called for Estrildis to be taken from the line of prisoners and he became her devoted lover. This was a good thing, and it would have been an even better thing if it wasn't for the fact that Locrinus was already promised in marriage to the daughter of an important family friend, a friend of his father's – a good strategic alliance. He was promised to Gwendolen, daughter of Cornicus. Now history has little to say about whether Gwendolen knew about Estrildis and if so what her feelings were on the matter. However, it seems that Cornicus took it as a personal insult. He insisted – and by insisted, I mean sharp blades and threats were involved – that Locrinus honour his promise, and marry Gwendolen. Which Locrinus did, without much complaint. He was, after all, both a lover and a fighter and sometimes strategic steps have to be taken to accommodate both these tendencies.

And so Locrinus and Gwendolen set up their home in a castle befitting their status. But Locrinus, the lover and fighter, and Estrildis, the high-born prisoner in a strange land, well, they were deep ones. What they had begun they did not choose to finish. When the wedding of Locrinus and Gwendolen was complete, Locrinus and Estrildis continued their lives together by going underground – quite literally. Estrildis set up her domain in a labyrinthine underground fortress of caves and once a year Locrinus came on a visit to stay with her. For seven years they lived in this way, and during those seven years Estrildis in her fortress beneath the ground bore a daughter named Habren, and Gwendolen in her castle above the ground bore a son named Maddan. And Maddan was sent to the court of his grandfather, Cornicus, to learn all that a boy who is destined to be king might need to know. And Habren remained with her mother Estrildis, in the labyrinthine fortress – and she learned many things. The ways of the turns of fortune, and the tides of chance, and the laws of cause and effect, and the way the light grows from darkness. She was a strange, quiet child, whose wisdom grew quickly, along with a certain restlessness …

But at the end of seven years, change came. Cornicus died. And Locrinus, perhaps thinking that he had so successfully combined the role of lover and fighter and husband that he could now afford to set the plates spinning again and still remain in control, brought Estrildis and Habren up from the labyrinthine fortress beneath the ground and openly revealed his love for them. Gwendolen acted swiftly. She called on the allegiance of her father's court and she raised a fighting force – possibly from Cornwall, possibly from Gwent – who marched against Locrinus and killed him in a battle near Stourport.

Estrildis once again found herself taken prisoner and this time by one who was not regarding her with the eyes of love. She and her young daughter were taken by Gwendolen on a forced march upriver all the way to Abermule, above Newtown, about fifty miles or so. And there they stopped. Perhaps by then Gwendolen had walked off the first of her fury. She and Estrildis regarded one another. And Gwendolen took hold of Habren and gave orders to her men to drive Estrildis away from her sight. Which they did, and what became of her then legend does not tell.

Gwendolen looked at the young girl, who backed off from her gaze, backed off all the way to the bank of the river. Still Gwendolen stood and stared at her, and in her heart feelings of hate and pity and longing and confusion were all fighting to be heard. Finding herself on the very edge of the river, the girl took another step and slithered down the bank, and began to wade into the water. She waded to the mid-point of the river, and stood there in the fast flow, her toes clinging to the stones of the riverbed, her legs wide, trying to balance, to stay upright in the quick, cold water, which came up to her chest. Gwendolen watched in surprise as the girl stood there in the water. As Habren shivered, rigid with cold in the river, so Gwendolen shuddered and shivered on the bank and they did not take their eyes off one another. Then pity and love gained the upper hand in Gwendolen's heart and she said to herself, 'I will raise her as my child in my court and I will have no other daughter than this.' She asked her name, and the girl replied – but in the very moment that Habren spoke her name, she vanished beneath the waves.

It was so quick that Gwendolen couldn't understand what had happened – the girl was there and then she was gone, down beneath the water. Gwendolen shouted and began looking, expecting at any moment for the small head to bob to the surface – but the sun was low and blinding on the river's surface and the trees cast dappled shadows. Once or twice she thought she caught a glimpse of a strand of hair or the fingers of a hand; she thought she saw the colour of the robe the girl was wearing, disappearing down the river. Gwendolen began to hurry along the riverbank, pushing through the trees, keeping her eyes fixed on the river. She called to her men to search, she sent them into the water, she sent them ahead to the bend in the river. But they saw nothing, though they searched for many days. And Gwendolen went on searching too, and some say that she never stopped searching … and so she passes out of our story.

Habren did not close her eyes as she sank below the water. Through the blur, she felt herself to be moving quite fast and quite easily, like floating or flying, for some time. On she flew, on a cold twisting journey with the river, and above her a silver light rose, the moon full and the water flooding. There were hands at her – touching her, guiding her in the flow. There were hands combing her hair as she travelled. There were mouths beside her ears, like fishes' mouths, but speaking sweetly of many things that only the river knows. Habren lingered a good while in a deep place, among whirls and eddies that seemed familiar. The girl who had grown up and played and taken her first footsteps in a labyrinth of earth, now moved in a quiet water-maze. As she had learned to trust the earth, now she learned to trust the water. And so in time the young girl became riverdaughter, sweetwater maiden. She became one with the river and its ways.

In due course the swirling River Severn widens. Salt water comes flooding through and around Habren the sweetwater maiden. And in the midst of that bold, briny rush and swirl, on a rolling wave like a rearing horse comes the one who some call Nudd, and some name Nodens. He comes wrapping his silver arms around her, bearing her up, holding, enfolding. And in his salt flood they travel together back upstream for a while, transported, tumbled in rough magic, leaping with the salmon.

Habren's home is here now, from the bubbling short grasses of stony Plynlimon to the bend at Chepstow and beyond. She is here, in this ribbon line of flow with its wide-muddied hem. Her lover's boisterous embrace returns to her regular as the tide, and by moonlight, sunlight or dark of night, they flow together, salt and sweet.

5

HERE I AM

Here is the beautiful carved head in the little church of St Jerome in Llangwm Ucha, and of course he is wreathed in leaves. He dreams very quietly and deep and long. Depending on the time of day (or night) you are visiting and how the light and shadow falls, it may be his lone face you see first or it may be the twinned dreaming heads nearby. It doesn't matter. All three are as deep and quiet as one another, and they are all at a different point in the same dream. It's just possible that you might pass by and never notice even one of his three stone faces. They're hidden in plain sight, as the saying goes; they were masters of that kind of hiding from the moment they were carved and by now they have had long centuries of practice. But if you are the right one (no telling who) at the right moment (no telling when) you will see this dreamer.

To hear him breathe, well, for that you have to be very still. You could begin by looking; open up the eyes of your eyes. Listen with your ears first then with the ears of your ears. Then, quieten down deep into your own breath and you may find yourself at the threshold of the dream, where he waits. Lots of people have found themselves at that threshold and known, just for an instant, that it is there for them alone. When Julia, Lady Raglan stood looking and listening and breathing she knew it too. The moment was hers, fresh and keen as a green blade splitting through rock. She looked and saw in his face fronds curling and leaf buds opening, deep and wild and strong and gentle, hardly held back by the stone. The look went both ways, of course. A twinkle from a stone eye to Julia's own, and one shared breath. Julia visited often, returning again and again to the quiet, vibrant threshold. She discovered, as many had before her, that when you are poised on that threshold, in the moment before you step over, the look from his eye and his curling breath can bring about a strange sort of wondering. For example, it might cross your mind, just momentarily, that the Virgin Mary conceived by listening to the angel, or that the breath of God breathes life into dust, or that the sun calls to the green shoot until it hears. In some way you may feel you have been touched – and something has quickened in you. And now you are fruitful indeed. You're someone you thought you had forgotten, someone you will now never be able to forget again. It occurred to Julia at that moment to name him the Green Man. What the Green Man called Julia when they passed time together there, no one can say. He may have called her to guess at her own names. That is a thing he does; calls to the bits of you that were you before your names and titles, roles and occupations, age and condition. The bit of you that belongs to the wild, to the whole – that is to say, all of you.

It's most likely that he called her by her summer names, as she had called his.

And once they had met and spoken their names at that threshold, the Green Man and Julia went bounding, springing, grasping hand and waist, leaping together into the intensely green surge and froth of the churchyard that circled them like a moat. Beyond the walls of the little church nestling beneath its tower, green rioted in various hues. Green threaded itself with primroses or bursting thistle-heads, depending on the season. Kestrels called, the stream chatted. The wind blew and fell still, many times over. The remembered and the forgotten dead sat in the sun or the shade, depending on their preferences. St Jerome wondered and was wondered at. Mirgint, Cinfice, Hui and Erneu, the early, earthy workers of simple miracles in that place, leaned back together against a beech tree and rested their bones and wondered about names and what a long, glorious kerfuffle it is, this business of forgetting and remembering.

When Julia sat at her desk, putting a little distance between herself and the look and the threshold and the green riot, she found herself thinking about the mason. She imagined how he must have exhaled clouds of moist breath on a winter morning as he worked, how his breath would have become entwined closer and closer with the wreathing stone leaves. She pictured how his hand had held the chisel and how long he must have had to keep his focus on that threshold, where she had only lasted an instant before she was pulled across and whirled away. How astonishing that the mason had held steady, holding the thought that must have filled his being; the knowledge that stone was bones, that spirit was substance, that stone leaves rustled and a carved smile widened. That the twinkle of a stone eye could deepen until you fell into it, and went dancing into summer.

Those leafy stone heads, hidden in plain sight. They were masters of that kind of hiding from the moment they were carved and by now they have had long centuries of practice. But if you are the right one (no telling who) at the right moment (no telling when) you will see these dreamers.

6

'UP I GO!'

Not far from Trellech, a labourer came tramping wearily along the lane just as dusk was falling. He was worn out by days on the road, traipsing from village to village in an unsuccessful search for work and he'd spent the last few nights under a hedge. He was hungry, he was thirsty and he was cold. He branched off from the lane to cut across a field and as he was plodding through the mud he spotted a little cottage stood on its own by a stand of trees.

He decided to chance his arm and see if whoever lived there would offer him a crust or a little shelter for the night. He knocked on the door, straightened his shoulders and waited. A woman came to the door quite quickly and stood there looking at him. The man muttered a few words but the woman said nothing. A little tabby cat came and sat at her feet and the cat and the woman both looked at the man without saying anything. After a few moments the man shrugged and was just turning away when the woman opened the door a little wider and gestured to him to come inside. So he did.

Very soon the man was sat by the embers of a fire with a bowl of broth to warm his hands and belly. He also had a cat to knead his thighs very thoroughly with all her claws, but that was a small inconvenience. Neither the man nor the woman were chatty types, so the evening passed quietly and when the woman saw his eyelids drooping she told him to go off upstairs to sleep in the only bed, since she and the little cat were just as happy by the fireside. The man had been the receiver of more kicks than ha'pennies in his life and he knew better than to turn down a generous offer, so he nodded his thanks and went straight up to bed as directed. He was asleep even before he had time to wonder whether there would be anything for breakfast.

Yes, he fell asleep straightaway – but before long he woke up even more suddenly. In the corner of the bedroom there was a small wooden chest, and by the light of the moon that was shining in through the thin curtains he saw that the woman had come into the room, lifted the lid of the chest and was searching for something inside. As he watched, the woman took a stout stick from the chest. The man clutched the blanket and held his breath, getting ready to leap up and defend himself. But the woman went quietly over to the window and opened the latch. Then she sat on the windowsill with her legs dangling outside and the stout stick still in her hand. She stayed poised there for a split second and then he heard her say quietly but clearly '*Up I go!*' – and she was gone; disappeared into the night. The man felt a wild surge of excitement. He jumped out of bed and ran to rummage in the wooden chest, where he soon found another stout stick. He ran to the window and got up on the ledge just as he had seen the woman do. And with scarcely a moment's hesitation he took firm hold of the stick and said '*Up I go!*', and he too disappeared off and away into the moonlit night.

Clinging on to the stout stick for dear life, the man found himself whizzing along above the treetops. He could see the woman some way ahead of him and he did his best to follow her. 'If I lose sight of her,' he thought to himself, 'then goodness knows where I will end up.' She seemed to be making for a little hill, where a large house stood. There were a couple of lamps still alight in an upstairs window and he realised with some surprise that he knew this place well enough; he'd tried to get work there several times and always been turned away at the door. The woman flew down and around the house to a little door at the back, which opened wide just as she approached. She seemed set to fly straight inside when suddenly she stopped and looked around sharply. Somehow, he just about managed to stop in time without crashing into her. Even through the darkness he could feel she was staring straight at him. It felt even more uncomfortable than the time before on her doorstep. Then at last she said '*In I go!*' and flew on into the house and he quickly said '*In I go!*' and flew in after her. Down the passageway they went and straight into the kitchen. There in the warmth and quiet, with all the household asleep upstairs, they helped themselves to bread and cheese and milk and cakes until they couldn't eat any more. Then the woman got to her feet and went over to a little door that led down to the cellar. She pointed her stick at the stone steps and said '*Down I go!*', and '*Down I go!*' he said, too. And down in the cellar they drank their fill of the finest wines and spirits. They drank and they laughed and they made very, very merry and it didn't matter at all that they weren't chatty types because soon they had no need of words at all.

Then suddenly in the very midst of their merrymaking there was a thud and a harsh shout. The master of the house was on a night prowl, and had spotted the door of the cellar ajar. He stood at the top of the stone steps and peered down. He roared to his servants to wake up and come and catch a rat. Trapped there beside the wine casks in the dark, the man turned to the woman, only to find that she was no longer at his side. It was as if she had simply melted away into the dark and he was alone, in the growing circle of light from the servants' candles.

In those times, the punishment for most kinds of theft was hanging. And having helped himself liberally to food from the kitchen and wine that he could not possibly pay for, the man was under no illusions that he would receive any kind of clemency whatsoever. In the dingy lock-up that served as a village gaol he awaited his fate, which seemed certain. And the day that the man was to be hanged duly arrived. As he was led out to the gibbet, a woman, cloaked and hooded, approached the hangman and begged leave to be allowed to have a final few words with her son. The man heard this request with some surprise, since his mother had been dead for a good many years. But the hangman nodded agreement, and when the woman approached the man, she stood looking at him from under her hood and said nothing. Then suddenly her fist shot out from under her cloak; she was clutching a stout stick. The man had just enough wits about him not to squander a generous offer and he too grabbed hold of the stick. The woman shouted '*Up we go!*' and up they both went, up and away, and there was no hanging that day.

7

GWARWYN-A-THROT

There was a woman, no one knew where she came from, but she came walking over the mountain one morning and reported for work at Pantygaseg farm in the parish of Mynyddislwyn. This was long ago, when there was a good scatter of little farms on the lower slopes where now there are mostly only bits of walls that the sheep get their backs against to rest and shelter.

Now, arriving from nowhere without a clear local pedigree is usually easier if you're young and pretty, which this woman was, and if you have a ready smile and a spring in your step, which she did. And from the very start she fitted right in to life on the farm and she did her work well, from dawn till dusk. At first it bothered people that they didn't know exactly where she came from or who her people were, only that her name was Jennet. At the root of the wondering was the thought that this quick, smiling young woman who had walked brightly out of the morning mist might in some way be connected to *Bendith y Mamau*: the Mothers' Blessing, the fair ones. One or two of the keener-eyed women thought there was a slight shimmer to be seen in the air when Jennet was at her work; a sense of excitement when there was no call for it. And it may be that the dust angels whirled a little brighter in the shafts of light when she swept the floor by the window. But really there was nothing much at all that anyone could have put their finger on. So the suspicion, the curiosity and the wondering diminished fairly quickly amongst the everyday busyness of farm life.

It might have been a different matter if they'd known how at ease Jennet was with the Pwca, who had arrived not long after her. Now, of course, everybody knew that there was no telling when a Pwca might turn up, and if and when one chose to live in your farm-house there was nothing you could do about it really. The presence of a Pwca was a mixed blessing. An absolute godsend with the daily chores, but very easy to offend, and an offended Pwca was NOT a good thing. Anyhow, there was Jennet and there, very soon after, was the Pwca and they got on very well indeed. It was as if they somehow understood one another and the Pwca behaved like a real little treasure. He finished many of the tasks that Jennet simply did not have time to do and he seemed to know instinctively just what things in particular she needed help with, or disliked doing. It was all rather harmonious. The Pwca moved around her unseen as she worked, watching, taking note and taking care not to get in the way, like a little invisible dance partner. In fact, if there was an instruction booklet as to how a helpful Pwca should behave, this Pwca must have read it. At night when everyone was asleep, he invisibly did all the work that still needed doing. And in time-honoured fashion every night before Jennet went to bed, usually last of all the servants, she left a bowl of warm milk with crusts soaking in it for the Pwca to eat. Every morning she got up first, with the morning star still bright in the sky, to tidy the empty bowl away. And so things continued for some time. And all was well and all was orderly at the farmhouse for a good long while.

Now Jennet had a bright, lively sense of humour. She was slow to complain and quick to laugh. Very quick. One morning, the boy from the fullers came round with a large pot collecting urine for the fleeces and when Jennet emptied the contents of her own pot in with the rest a thought came to her that made her laugh out loud, and she kept back a ladleful. That night, in the bowl that she usually filled with milk and soaking crusts for the Pwca, Jennet emptied the contents of the ladle, with a twist of sheep's fleece soaking in it. She left the bowl at the foot of the stair as normal and went on up to bed. It was a child's joke, really – an April fool, in the spirit of mischief. So when the Pwca finished his night's work he took up the bowl and supped up a large mouthful of piss and wool, and he gagged and spat and retched.

When Jennet came stepping down just before first light next morning, the Pwca was waiting. Then those two did not move around the farmhouse in a discreet and harmonious dance, no, far from it. Instead it was more like a hot and hard Argentinian tango, rough love only with no words, no music, one unwilling and one invisible partner. A chair was flung and cracked against a wall, a lamp spilled grease.

'*There was no need of it!*' the Pwca hissed at Jennet. She had had her fun and now he was having his. But Jennet was lively – even at that time of the morning. Fast on her feet, hard to catch hold of, but catch her he did at last. He grabbed and twisted the skin on her wrist till it burned, then he held her in his two scrawny arms, fought, bit, punched her belly, kicked her between her legs. Jennet cried out for help, again and again, but no one came. They didn't want to. They heard the screams and the crashes and thuds as if in a dream, and they hid from what they heard, under the blankets.

Dawn was just breaking when Jennet went walking away over the hill into the morning mist. A couple of the milkmaids saw her and thought for a moment that her skin was purple with bruises, but it was probably just a trick of the morning light. It was the last any of them saw of Jennet – if that really was her name.

But a Pwca will not fade away so easily. A Pwca must always find a place to be – a household to be part of. But he can't just set out in search of somewhere – no, a Pwca must hitch a lift, or be carried in some way, unbeknown to the carrier. And so he began to look out for a suitable opportunity. Within a day or so the Pwca noticed that a milkmaid named Margret had come from Hafod-yr-ynys to fetch a jug of barm for the baking. When he saw her walking carefully back across the farmyard with her precious jugful he said quietly, *'The Pwca is going away now in this jug of barm and he will never come back.'*

And so it was. Unbeknown to Margret, she carried the Pwca back to Hafod-yr-ynys in the jug.

Now, there was nothing misty or fading about Margret. She was solid and real, not a spring in her step but a roll in her stride and when she hugged you, you knew about it. And Margret was a hard worker. It was a little while before she realised the Pwca was living in her farmhouse, but she knew that on the odd occasion when she left work unfinished, someone was finishing it for her and more besides. And eventually she put two and two together, and she started to leave a bowl of milk and crusts at night and there we are. Of course, the Pwca was as invisible to Margret as he ever had been to Jennet, but anyway Margret had weak eyes, and this was in the days before reliable spectacles. However, Margret had an excellent ear. She was in the habit of listening to things – the milk in the pail, the bellows breath of the cows. She also had a beautiful voice. She praised her heart out on a Sunday, and throughout the week she hummed and sang as she worked. The Pwca found it not unpleasant to listen to her.

When the evenings were lighter Margret would settle to some spinning, but she didn't really care for this work because it strained her eyes. Still she managed well enough, setting up a rhythm with the turning of the wheel, click and whirr, click and whirr. But she was very pleased to find that the Pwca positively excelled at spinning. So she began to leave out heaps of fleece in a basket beside her wheel, which she set by the embers of the fire at night, and she would sometimes lie quietly in the time between sleeping and waking, listening to the steady, pleasant rhythm of the Pwca spinning. Click and whirr … click and whirr … a soothing sound to fall asleep to. But one full moon, Margret did not fall asleep as she lay listening to the click and whirr. Instead she crept out onto the stairs and sat and watched and listened. There was the Pwca crooning peacefully to himself as he played the fleece between his fingers and the wheel turned; it was a gentle, lilting mantra: '*Gwarwyn-a-Throt-I-am, Gwarwyn-a-Throt-I-am, Gwarwyn-a-Throt …*'

A perfect rhythm, over and over. It was a peaceful, intimate moment there in the quiet of the night, with the silver moon at the window and the embers red in the hearth, and as Margret sat listening on the stair she joined in dreamily … '*Gwarwyn-a-Throt-I-am, Gwarwyn-a-Throt …*'

The moment the Pwca heard Margret's voice he stopped dead. The wheel spun, the fleece fell from his hands. The Pwca was on his feet in an instant and bounding across the floor. Margret was still sat halfway up the stairs so the Pwca could not quite reach her, but he stretched up as high as he could and with his eyes smouldering he craned his long white neck and hissed and spat at her, called her Lousy Lardarse, Stinking Splitarse – a dozen filthy names. He cursed and he swore right in Margret's face and though he could not lay a finger on her, the names he called hurt her. They did.

Margret reflected a few days later, as she sat with her head resting against a cow's flank, listening to the rhythmic ssshhhh and froth of the milk squirting into the pail, that she had not meant to find out the Pwca's name, or say it aloud. She hadn't even been trying to guess it. She had just joined in his song for a moment, because it was so nice … so peaceful … just him at the wheel and her on the stair. After that, she never did speak his name again, not to anyone, though it was always there at the back of her mind. Only when she was very old and her grandchildren played around her did she mention it to one of them, who remembered and told it one day to their own grandchildren, which I suppose is how I can tell you now.

The Pwca had been truly shocked to hear his name spoken. So shocked that if he could have chosen, he would never have set foot in a human habitation again. But he could not choose. He did, however, make a rather bold move. He went to live in a farmhouse where there were no women, just a widowed farmer and a few male servants, who shared the work between them. He had to bide his time, of course, waiting for the opportunity, but it soon came, when a little girl was given a basket of newly wound balls of yarn to take to the Trwyn farm on the other side of the hill. The basket was quite big and the girl was quite small and as she struggled down the path the Pwca spotted his chance and murmured, '*I am going away now in this ball of wool and I will never come back.*'

When the little girl stumbled on a stone on the ridge of the hill, the ball containing the Pwca fell out of the basket and rolled all the way down to the Trwyn farm. There, since a Pwca's job is to assist where assistance is needed, he attached himself to the head servant, whose name was Moses. From the moment Moses realised the Pwca was there, the two of them got along very well – though not quite in the way the Pwca was used to. For one thing, Moses seemed to think nothing of speaking directly to him, almost as if he was another farmhand! Quite early on, Moses astonished the Pwca by suddenly stopping in his tracks and saying, 'Pwca, have you milked the cows?'

The Pwca was so wrongfooted at being suddenly spoken to, and in broad daylight, that he just said, 'Yes I have! Are you doubting me?'

To which Moses replied, stoutly, 'Yes I am.'

Then, when ten minutes later Moses found the full churns and apologised to the Pwca for his mistake, the Pwca was quite won over. After that Moses spoke clear and plain to the Pwca whenever there was something that needed saying, and the Pwca would say a word or so in reply – not that you would call it a conversation, but words were exchanged between the two of them, and they became as good friends as it is possible for a farm servant and a Pwca to be. Even when the farmer installed his new wife at the Trwyn farm, things continued amicably for a good many years.

But here this particular Pwca's story takes an odd little twist; it gets pinned to an exact date, which is the 22nd of August 1485. Because the thing that made the Pwca and Moses fall out at last was that Moses decided to go marching off to the Battle of Bosworth, away in Leicestershire. The Pwca had no interest whatsoever in wars, and since he had found the only person who came remotely close to what you might call a friend, he did a very un-Pwca-like thing and he actually made himself visible, got down on his knees and begged Moses not to go. Moses was disconcerted, and a bit embarrassed, and once he had shaken the Pwca free from his knees he took down his coat from the peg and left that very day. Moses favoured Henry 'the Welshman' over Richard III any day of the week – or at least his masters did. And away at the Battle of Bosworth, Henry won the day and the crown, and Moses lost his life.

When the news got back to the farm, the Pwca was wretched. And he did what we already know from this story that he had a tendency to do when he felt hurt or threatened, he struck out. He turned to Pwca tricks. He goaded the oxen with sharpened sticks, so they halted and fretted in the furrows, he spilt milk pails, kicked hens, broke china, scuffed up new-planted seeds, and hid things when they were most needed. The farmer's wife knew perfectly well that this was a Pwca's doing, and she explained it to the farmer, and the two of them tried to persuade the Pwca to mend his ways. They tried bribing him, they tried threatening him, and when nothing they said or did made the slightest bit of difference, in desperation they went off to Caerleon, to seek advice from the *dyn cynnil*, who was reputed to have experience with Pwcas.

The wise man reassured the distracted farmer and his wife that he could help them, and promised to come to their farm on the night of the next full moon, which he did. He sat by the fire and sniffed the air and waited very still for a moment, then he made a lunge and a grab at what seemed to the farmer and his wife to be nothing but empty air, but soon revealed itself to be the Pwca. There he was, forced into shape between the wise man's clenched fists – a little, wretched figure, glaring and miserable, held tightly by the nape of his long white neck and the tip of his long nose.

The Pwca hung limply while the *dyn cynnil* intoned a long, winding spell, ending with the following words:

And you shall be taken to the very shores of the Red Sea where you will dwell for fourteen generations, and the wind that shall carry you there will be the bold wind, the upper wind and it will come for you NOW!

And it came, the rushing, howling *uwchwynt*, that made the whole farmhouse shudder, and it plucked the Pwca from between the wise man's hands and carried him up and away to the banks of the Red Sea. The Pwca was not seen again, and the farmhouse settled down into peace and quiet for a time.

By my reckoning, though, those fourteen generations have come and gone, so the Pwca may already have returned and may be in need of a household to join …

8

THE PROPHET

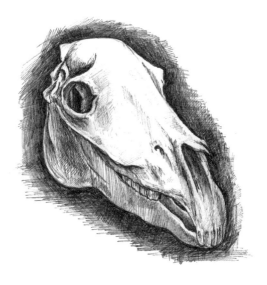

The Reverend Edmund Jones was an independent minister for most of his long life, which spanned the eighteenth century. And he lived for the most part of it in the north-west corner of Monmouthshire, in the parish of Aberystruth. His 'square mile' was dearest to him, though he travelled vigorously and deter-minedly on preaching tours until he was an old man; at the age of eighty he covered four hundred miles on foot through North Wales, preaching twice a day. But his field of enquiry, his field of dreams, was vast.

Edmund Jones was a great listener. He listened to places, to people, to rumours, to the wind in the leaves, the cawing of crows and the word of the Holy Spirit. He was a watcher, too. His was a time before industry burned over the valleys and dug into the hills. It was a quieter, more transparent time, when the fairy tribe, *Bendith y Mamau*, were heard and seen by many – though not by all. As a young boy Edmund had seen so clearly with his own eyes and experienced the strangeness of how things may be hidden in plain sight. And even as he saw, he understood how not all that seems clear enough is indeed visible to everybody. He was walking quite early one morning with his Aunt Elizabeth, his mother's sister, back home to Pen y Llwyn when, crossing a particular field Edmund saw a sheep fold with its door to the south. Over the doorway to the fold, in place of a lintel, was something that looked like a branch of a hazel tree. Many people were coming and going through the doorway, ducking their heads a little as they passed under the hazel branch. They were fair people, who seemed to Edmund to have been dancing and playing music, and many of them sat down inside the walls of the fold. He noted many little details – the men wore white cravats and he could pick out in particular a beautiful woman in a red jacket and high crown hat, whose pale face he never forgot. But his aunt made no comment at all on the strange sight, and when at last Edmund plucked up the courage to say what he had seen, he was amazed to find out that Aunt Elizabeth had seen nothing, and was reluctant to believe him.

Yes, when Edmund Jones watched, he sometimes noticed what others did not, and when he listened, he may not always have heard quite what others heard. But he was very interested in what his fellow parishioners had to say on such matters and he noted their comments down for reference. (Although he seemed to be quite afraid of the hold the devil had over old women, so he missed a lot of what they might have had to say. Which is a pity.) Many of his acquaintances had heard fairy music and Edmund noted that they all agreed that it was low and pleasing, though none could ever learn the tune. Others had had first-hand encounters with phantom funeral processions, which was one of the strange yet quite frequent ways that the fairy tribe revealed their presence to the people of the parish. Edmund felt that, since *Bendith y Mamau* thronged funeral processions so regularly and in such numbers, flanking the coffin on all sides as it progressed towards the churchyard, it must mean that they knew in advance when a death would take place and were ready for it. Edmund felt certain that they knew this because they understood the stars and their influence more deeply than people did. They had knowledge of how the wheel of time turned. Though why they appeared and disappeared in that way, and what they meant by it was not easy to understand. Edmund's own school teacher, Howel Prosser, a curate of the parish, had himself seen a funeral going down the lane one evening towards the church and had presumed the coffin held the body of a certain man from the north of the parish. He hurried to help the bearers, as was the custom when the coffin had been carried a long distance, but when he stretched out his hand the whole procession instantly vanished into the thin evening air – and Howel Prosser was left cradling in his arms the skull of a horse.

Now, Edmund didn't approve of the fairies – but he didn't doubt that they existed, and that they knew things. I imagine that he would have been horrified to be compared to the fairies in any way – but the fact is that one of the things people came to notice about Edmund was that he did seem to know things before they happened. For example, when asked to preach at a particular meeting or event he might answer, 'I cannot, on that day; the rain will descend in torrents, and there will be no congregation.'

And he would be absolutely right. Or he would give his coat and his last penny to the needy and assure his wife that she should not be anxious, because a messenger would arrive with food and raiment at nine o'clock the next day – and there the helpful messenger would be, at the predicted hour. And, perhaps in keeping with the view that the Lord helps those who help themselves, Edmund's friends and household were ready with their support, and so too were his parishioners. And since Edmund only took a very small salary for his ministry, a farm servant from the Tranch would go to Pontypool on market day and stand outside the old Corn Market where she would lay a basket on the ground and simply announce that she was the servant of the Reverend Edmund Jones. By the end of the day the basket would be filled with eggs, cheese and other provisions that people had willingly gifted to the minister.

But if Edmund was known as a fine preacher, a kind man and a proven prophet, his kindness and his gift of prophesy could sometimes take challenging forms.

Just over the border in Llangattock, two farmers had separately offered a plot of land for the building of a new chapel and there was disagreement among the congregation as to which offer to accept. A general cooling of relations had resulted, so much so that before long a central aisle was put in the barn where the congregation were temporarily worshipping and the different factions sat on either side. When Edmund Jones' opinion was sought to break the deadlock, he was unimpressed.

'Appeal to me?' he roared. 'Never mind about appealing to me, what about appealing to the Almighty?'

Then he strode down the aisle sternly enquiring, 'Beth yw'r ymrannu yma?' ('What is all this separation?')

The congregation, somewhat shamefacedly, were soon on their knees on the bare floor of the barn with instructions to stay there until Jones 'received a revelation'. He kept them there for an hour and a quarter. Then he called out an abrupt 'Follow me!' and strode out of the barn. The congregation staggered stiffly to their feet and went hobbling after him, blinking in the bright sunlight.

They followed him up the hill for half a mile, then back down again. They paused and waited expectantly; might now be the time for an adjudication? But no, Jones simply turned on his heel and set off for a second time back up the hill – and then back down again. The congregation dug deep and kept up as best they could. After the second descent, one of them managed to summon up the courage to ask when they might expect a judgement. The reply came: 'When I receive a sign, and not before!' and off up the hill again went Edmund Jones, and off up the hill went the congregation too, and then back down for a third time. It may well have been an occasion very like this one that gave rise to the perpetual round, 'A man climbed up a mountain, a man climbed up a mountain ...' with its never-ending cycle of ascents and descents.

But of course, there is an end to everything eventually and this marathon ended in style. On the fourth ascent, Jones paused for a moment in contemplation. He pulled his coat tightly around him and rested on his staff. The congregation stood panting and wheezing like an orchestra of poorly maintained concertinas. At last, when all was stillness and mountain hush, as Jones continued to stand there in contemplation, a starling flew down from a nearby tree and perched solemnly on his shoulder. Then Edmund Jones announced to the intrigued circle of the faithful that the new chapel should be built in that very spot. It is said that a member of the group who owned the particular piece of land was present, and donated it then and there. And then the Prophet and the starling and the entire congregation made their ways home.

Edmund Jones lived in a world that was about to change very fast. In fact, the change had already begun, and the land was illuminated now not just by moonlight but by 'the light of the Gospel' as Nonconformism took hold, driving out the fairy folk and belief in them. And when the furnace fires of the Industrial Revolution began to light up the day and the night skies, you would have to look much harder and listen much more patiently to glimpse the Bendith y Mamau or to hear their music.

9

TREDUNNOCK

The star-browed ox that Gwynllyw followed and the sow Hen Wen who farrowed on the shore were part of a much larger to-ing and fro-ing of beasts and people making their way across the pleasant land of Gwent. Cows and pigs, salmon and eagles, saints, queens, dairymaids, warriors and poets moved across this land with their routes, their rhymes, their reasons that change in the telling.

Cadoc, the saintly son of Gwynllyw and Gwladys, had left his monastery away in Llancarfan for a while and was living at his house of prayer near Caerleon when a man rode up one misty morning and asked to be given refuge. The man's name was Ligessawc Law Hir (Ligessawc Long Hand), and although he had been a leader of men, right now he was a fugitive. Everywhere he went he was hunted. There was a price on his head and he was forced to be always on the move, sleeping in ditches, under hedges, wherever he could. He was being hunted with great tenacity because he had killed three men, and not just any men – Arthur's men. Almost everyone seemed to know that Ligessawc was on the run from Arthur and they didn't want to get involved. So no one offered Ligessawc very much in the way of help, apart from surreptitiously slipping him the odd bit of bread. Although nobody who caught a glimpse of him was in any hurry to go and report him to Arthur's men, they were in no hurry to offer him shelter either. They just hoped he would move on, fast. And Ligessawc Law Hir had been moving on and moving on and now the autumn days were lengthening and he was running out of options. So he had made a last throw of the dice and he knocked on the door of Cadoc, whose reputation for holiness and wisdom had already spread far and wide. And when he came face to face with Ligessawc there at the door, looking him right in the eyes and requesting refuge, Cadoc asked him to tell his story. So Ligessawc told his version of events, his account of why he was a fugitive. He spoke briefly, because he was a man of few words, and when Cadoc had heard what he had to say, his response was equally brief and to the point. He said 'Enter.'

And so to his great relief, Ligessawc received shelter and sustenance at the house of prayer with Cadoc and a small group of Cadoc's brothers in God, and it was nobody else's business. And so it continued for some time. Ligessawc certainly wasn't a free man but at least he wasn't sleeping in a muddy ditch in constant fear for his life. However, there in Caerleon he was more or less right under Arthur's nose; it was really only a matter of time before word came to Arthur that the man he had been hunting the length and breadth of the land was holed up just down the road, being given sanctuary in the house of prayer. Now, it was a close contest in many ways as to who had most clout, Arthur or Cadoc, and I don't know whether it was that Arthur didn't want to put it to the test, or whether it came from a deep respect for the sanctuary of the holy house, but although Arthur could have gone steaming in and claimed Ligessawc and flattened the house of prayer with no difficulty, he didn't do that. Instead, Arthur took a good number of his troops down to the banks of the River Usk and he sent word to Cadoc to come to a parley and explain himself. And Arthur and his troops set up quite a pleasant makeshift camp on the banks of the Usk and they settled down in the autumn sunshine to wait for Cadoc to arrive.

Now, to give Ligessawc Law Hir his due, when he saw Arthur's messenger arrive and he heard the summons he said to Cadoc, 'Look, this summons is really for me. You have treated me with honour and you have kept your word. It's true what people say about you, you're a wise and good man. Now it's up to me to go and face Arthur.'

And it may have been that Cadoc, touched by those words, felt more determined than ever to protect this man, or he may have secretly been waiting for just such a chance to lock horns with Arthur. But however it was, when Ligessawc had finished speaking Cadoc said, 'Do as I tell you and stay here.'

Then Cadoc and a few of his brothers in God went down to the river and he stood looking over at Arthur's men on the far bank. And Arthur and his men stood looking over at them, and for a while no one said anything and there was no sound except for the occasional whinnying of one of the horses and the murmuring of the river. At last Arthur called out to Cadoc and asked if it was true that he was harbouring the fugitive Ligessawc Law Hir and Cadoc replied, 'Yes.' Arthur said, 'Oh.' Then for a moment he didn't say anything else at all, because he wasn't really sure what to say. Arthur's men and Cadoc's men all wondered what was going to happen next. It was a stand-off. For a few moments, you could have heard an autumn leaf drop. Then a heated conversation began to be shouted back and forth. Arthur insisted that Cadoc give up the fugitive immediately; Cadoc said that it was a right for anyone who sought sanctuary in the house of prayer to be granted their request. Arthur demanded that Ligessawc Law Hir face the consequences of his actions immediately and that Cadoc might have to do so as well at this rate. Cadoc replied that he made a point of never giving in to threats. Arthur claimed he was owed justice, Cadoc counter-claimed that holy sanctuary meant holy sanctuary and there was nothing anyone could do about it. And on it went, all across the steady murmur of the river.

As the day wore on and the horses on Arthur's side of the river began to get a little restless, and the men on both sides were still wondering whether they were going to be splashing across the ford or not, Cadoc came up with a suggestion. He called over to Arthur, 'Since our views on this matter are not going to be easily reconciled, let us seek elsewhere for wisdom,' and he proposed that they appoint an independent panel of judges to decide which one of them was in the right. 'And whatever they decide,' said Cadoc, 'I will agree to abide by their verdict if you will agree likewise.'

Arthur took a few moments to discuss this suggestion with his brothers in arms Cai and Bedwyr, who were part of the company on that day, and the matter was agreed. With a bit of calling back and forth across the river they made a list of local wise men who could be found quickly and a scouting party of Arthur's men and Cadoc's men were sent off to round them up. Eventually they got back with a hastily assembled panel of local judges, some of whom stood on one bank and some on the other, and they debated the merits of the case. They debated for a long time; all night, and into the following morning. As the second day wore on Arthur's patience was getting stretched to breaking point and, sensing that their time was up, the judges announced that they had reached agreement on a decision. Their verdict was that the most fitting redress for Ligessawc's crime was not his life but a payment of one hundred cows and that this payment should be made at once, or else Ligessawc's life really would be forfeit.

When the verdict was delivered there was another of those silences, just the river murmuring, until Arthur said, 'Very well. I accept the verdict.' Cadoc said the same. Those of Arthur's men who had been looking forward to a bit of a skirmish sighed with frustration and those who had just been looking forward to getting back home to their dinner sighed with relief. And Cadoc's men were just about to go and start rounding up the cows when Arthur called out, 'Though, of course, they will have to be the best cattle. Red in front, white behind. You know the ones I'm talking about.'

They did know, of course. And they realised in an instant what Arthur had done. White cattle with red ears or red faces belonged to the times before. They came from the otherworld fairy cattle that were more highly prized than gold. To find one now would be a once-in-a-lifetime stroke of luck; to find a hundred was beyond anyone's wildest dreams. Arthur knew this as well as they did. Cadoc's men all turned and looked at Cadoc, and for a moment he seemed to hesitate. He stood watching the gently eddying water of the river, deep in thought. Then he gave a brisk nod to his little group of men and said, 'Go. Don't delay. Bring one hundred heifers to this place as has been requested, red before and white behind, and do not linger.'

And off went Cadoc's men to the fields and byres to locate and requisition one hundred non-existent fairy cattle. But as they trudged through the fields, every ordinary dun-coloured or mottled heifer that lay chewing the cud rose to its feet as they approached and stood quietly waiting. And not knowing what else to do, Cadoc's men began to herd them back towards the river. As they did so, the flanks of each cow began to change colour and by the time they reached the river the little group of men were leading a relaxed, mildly inquisitive herd of one hundred heifers, each one red in front and white behind.

A gasp rose from the far banks. Arthur's men were impressed. This was a phenomenal result. There then followed a bit of excitement and palaver about how exactly the handover of the cattle was to be made. It was decided to move a short way downstream to where there was a decent ford, where Cadoc's men would drive the heifers into the middle of the river and Arthur's men would wade in and take charge of steering the cows up onto the bank on their side. It proved easy enough to get the cattle into the shallows – they were already jostling for the water. Once in, however, the cows stopped and stood, enjoying the feel of the cool water on their legs and looking dreamily around them, as the leaves fell golden from the trees into the river's flow. Amongst general excitement a band of Arthur's men waded in to hurry the cows on across the ford and up the gently sloping bank on their side, but this was not so easy. They called and whooped and goaded and coaxed, but the cows would not budge. Then Cai and Bedwyr rolled up their sleeves and waded in to take charge and *they* whooped and goaded and coaxed, but still the cattle stood midstream, their feet planted firmly on the riverbed, enjoying the rush of the water and the unexpected turn their day had taken. Before long Cai and Bedwyr were red-faced and panting and had resorted to throwing their arms around the cows' necks in an attempt to heave them bodily onto the bank. At last, one cow took a step and began to amble slowly on and the rest followed suit. Arthur's men hastily scrambled forwards to help wrangle the cows to land. And as the cows were shoved and heaved onto the bank, each man found that in his arms he held not the thick, strong neck of a red-eared heifer but a bundle of ferns – and between their hands were not curling horns but bracken fronds. As Arthur looked on, the whole of the riverbank filled with bundles of fern until every last cow, red before and white behind, had disappeared.

It was suddenly cool there on the bank. After the first few shouts of surprise, utter silence fell. Cadoc and his men looked on, their faces pale as moth wings. Arthur himself went down on his knees in the fallen leaves and began to pray. He didn't know what had happened but he knew that something had taken its course and he had enough wisdom to know that it was not time to speak or remonstrate but to leave that place. Something was finished. When Arthur could get to his feet he nodded briefly over at Cadoc, who raised his hand and made a sign of blessing. Without a word, the men turned and followed Arthur away from the river, away through the trees, away back home. This business was at an end.

Cadoc sent his own men away with a word. Then he too fell to his knees, trembling uncontrollably. His teeth chattered too much for him to be able to utter a prayer even if one had come to his heart, which it did not. He half crawled, half stumbled down to the water's edge, let his hands hang in the water, his fingers grasping handfuls of riverbed shingle till they were numb with cold. The river's song was louder, louder than he had ever heard it before. Louder, deeper, older and harder to follow. He no more understood what had happened than Arthur did. Cadoc closed his eyes and let the Usk song flow through him until at last a prayer came, word by word, woven into the song. Only then did he open his eyes. A few dun-coloured heifers were wandering down the far bank into the water. One after another they rose from the fern bundles, regained their limbs, made their way steadily back across the ford, only stopping for a moment to drink, then on up the bank and back to their own fields, their waiting byres. They took no notice at all of Cadoc, who still knelt there, his hands dangling in the water, his fingers clutching handfuls of cold shingle.

Cadoc, Arthur, Ligessawc and their men are long gone. Generations of cattle of all colours have passed through the fields and byres, though red before and white behind are hardly ever seen. Only the river still runs. Today, the place where these events unfolded is called Tre Rhedynog. Ferny Town. Tredunnock.

THE WHITSON HENWIFE

The Whitson henwife was young. Younger than you might think, anyway, if your idea of henwives is that they are quite wise and very wrinkly. Her husband was away making shoes for much of the time and she lived with her little daughter, a yard full of chickens and a well-stocked and tended garden. She was prone to bursting into song, usually making the words up as she went along.

The Whitson henwife loved lots of things, which is usually a good sign. She loved catkins, and she brought them into the house and sat them in a jar by the window. If anyone else had done this, the villagers would have thought it was courting disaster, especially since they had noticed that she also picked bunches of snowdrops and brought them into the house too. Yes! Arranged them in a little bowl on the table with a pillow of moss and a twist of ivy … but, under the circumstances, they cautiously suspended judgement. After all, the henwife knew a few things that they didn't – that had been clear from the moment she and Will had come strolling into the village, newlywed. People had seen the way the speckled hen was tucked into the crook of her arm, and the way she nodded and straightened her skirt and the little sign she made as she stepped over the threshold of the cottage at the end of the lane. And from the first, the women and most of the men who expressed an opinion agreed that her advice had been sound on many things. What's more, she had usually been on hand and the door ajar and when she had no advice or opinion she listened and shared a piece of cake, which was often just as useful.

The henwife had a dozen speckled hens, and a few more with a lovely golden glint to their feathers in the sunlight, she thought. It goes without saying that hers were the healthiest and the most plentiful layers in the neighbourhood. And the cockerel was splendid, his comb scarlet as a fine lady's lips, and he could strut from dawn to dusk.

The henwife's daughter was a sturdy little girl, between two and three years old, who was usually to be found toddling along after her mother. In the morning she would dip her arm up to the shoulder into the corn sack and pull out podgy fistfuls of corn, which she flung haphazardly into the air with remarkable force for her age, and the hens went scurrying in all directions to peck up their breakfast wherever it may have landed.

Once, when her daughter's baby curls had begun to grow a little longer, the henwife had tied them up with a faded pink ribbon she had found snagged on a thorn. The little girl insisted on keeping the ribbon in her hair day and night and when it went missing she set up an ear-splitting wail – but luckily they found it in the first place they looked, which was, of course, the henhouse. There was the ribbon lying in the dirt, being pecked up and dropped, pecked up and dropped by one hen after another, who thought for a split second that they had found a super-long worm then quickly realised their mistake. The ribbon was back in the little girl's hair without even being swilled in water.

The henwife was often to be found carrying a hen under her arm or sat with one on her lap, if it was off-colour or if its legs were scaly – or sometimes for no real reason at all. Her little daughter chased, grabbed and cuddled hens almost as big as herself as soon as she could toddle after them. Mother and daughter alike chatted to the chickens quite regularly, in ways sometimes fantastical and sometimes matter-of-fact, in poetry and in prose, in good sense and in nonsense, in Welsh and in English. Listening to her daughter in conversation with a speckled broody, the henwife was fairly sure that although henwifery isn't strictly hereditary, this time it would be.

One January after their winter respite the hens had begun to lay again on the third day of the new year, as they always did. Deep within them they sensed the lengthening moments of light, heard the whisper to begin again, begin again. The henwife heard it too, in her own way. Whether the weather be wet, or whether the weather be dry, whether it be cold or colder, the light is returning, begin again. And always when she found the first egg of the new year lying on the straw the henwife's heart skipped in gladness and gratitude. Begin again even with no spring in sight yet, under heavy January skies. Bring a dish of snowdrops in for the table, never mind if people said it was unlucky. Begin again, begin again.

When the wall of water roared in across the fields that morning it swept the henhouse away, of course. The dog running to the house from the yard was engulfed by a curling wave. The henwife stood in the doorway, not understanding what she was seeing. She watched for the length of a breath, two breaths, and saw hens, pigs, dog, garden, walls and bushes vanish. The she turned back into the house, picked up her daughter, who lay curled up napping soundly on the bench, and hurried in the only direction she could – up the rickety ladder that led to a little low room where a wide beam jutted out a foot or so below the ceiling. She reached up and sat the child on the beam – propped her there, still bleary eyed and fuddled, only half-woken from her sleep. The blanket she had been wrapped in slipped into the water, which was already at the henwife's waist. With instructions to her child not to move, the henwife turned and made her way back down the stairs through the foaming, surging water. A hen came squawking crazily, flapping past her, its body squeezed into the last foot or so of air between the rising water and the ceiling. For a moment she felt its wing brush against her face. By the time she reached the foot of the stairs there was no tunnel of air at all above the henwife's head, and she lost her footing and went swirling, spinning, down and away …

A boat came after a day or so, when the waters lay still, manoeuvring cautiously through the now submerged everyday world of farms and cottages. At the henwife's cottage they peered in through the tiny upstairs window and there, perched on a beam they saw a little girl in a thin woollen petticoat with a draggled pink ribbon in her hair and her arms around a large speckled hen that sat quietly on her lap. 'It's what saved her life,' they always said, 'stuck there in the January cold in her nothings – that hen, puffing and plumping itself up like a feather blanket to keep the little one warm.'

I don't know for certain if the little girl grew to be a henwife. But she grew. Her mother's body was never found, and the little girl didn't remember much about her. Just how she told stories fantastical and practical, and said that there was no need to be worried about bringing catkins or snowdrops into the house, if you liked them.

11

TREACLE

When I was five, the buttercups at Usk Island grew higher than my head and walking through them I arrived at the water's edge shiny from head to toe with golden dust. Usk Island is a riverside water meadow, a magical place, as old water meadows often are. But there are also a couple of sea islands that are part of the story of the land of Gwent. There is tiny Denny island, whose shore marks the boundary of England and Wales, and there is also Chapel Rock. Chapel Rock is a tidal island, just about accessible at low tide, though in days gone by it was less cut-off. It is a liminal place, situated at the confluence of the Wye and the Severn in a stretch of water known as 'The Treacles'. It was a place of meetings, exchanges, and crossovers, long before the days of a bridge or a tunnel or even a reliable ferry. The dark, ragged promontory rock draws the eye and perhaps it always has. And where the eye is drawn, the footsteps of some may follow; and they may stay and make their abode there at that jagged edge.

Someone who did just that was a woman named Tecla. She lived in the fourth or maybe the fifth century and she was the daughter of a well-to-do Romano–British family away to the north in Gwynedd. When Tecla grew to womanhood, she named Christ as her true soul's companion and took the path of the early wandering saints of the Celtic lands. She went a-roaming, down through the middle of Wales all the way to the sea, where she stopped. There's no story of her following a star-browed ox, or a farrowing sow, or the flight of a crane – so perhaps she just followed her own footsteps until, at the far end of the land of Gwent, she saw the two great rivers swirling grey-brown and grey-blue into the Channel, the sun low over the water and the black rocks pushing up against the waves. And she went stepping out over the damp mud and grit, finding a shoulder of stone to shelter from the wind and a spring of water, clear and cold, life's mainstay. There she built her cell, raised her song to the salt winds. There she tended the well, made her home.

But anyone who had set up in that place would soon have been spotted. When people came to know that she was there, a little apart but set to stay, she must have had to hold her newly found ground with some determination. She must have planted her feet firmly on that rock so as not to get swept away by the first winds, the first questions, the first encounters. And before long people said, 'Yes. Here you are, praying and watching in this place to which our eyes are drawn.' And they took a blessing where they found one, and accepted a gulp from her well, and they found that the water was good, and eased them. And in time they came bringing her a fat salmon in fair exchange for a good blessing, because they considered the woman on the rock to be a mercy.

Still, to weave a story we have to darn a patch because Tecla's story on Chapel Rock was worn away long ago. Now it has just one little twisted thread fluttering at the edge – which is that Tecla was killed there on her island by pirates. Perhaps they were Saxons on a raiding trip in the Bristol Channel, perhaps not. Whoever they were, their act of murder of a lone woman was an old, old act that has been given a brand-new label. Tecla had named Christ as her true soul's companion and her murder made her the first known female Christian martyr in Britain.

Tecla shares a name with one of the shining women of the early Christian Church, and may well have been named after her; Saint Thecla who faced martyrdom several times and each time made a miraculous escape. She was tied to a pole in an amphitheatre to be burned alive, but was saved by a sudden hailstorm. She was ordered to be torn apart by beasts – devoured by a lion, drawn between bulls, but she was saved. A group of men then came to rape her and she fled – a rock opened up to facilitate her escape and she was never seen again. That is the story of the remarkable escaping Saint Thecla as it appears in Apocryphal texts. But as for her namesake Tecla on her sea-rock in Gwent, where the rivers meet and flood-tides roll by … if we want a story that will set her running free, we'll have to tell it ourselves, since legends are gone. We could give her a boat of her own, and watch her taking the rudder at a time of her own choosing. There she goes, bobbing away one morning to who knows where, bright eyes and busy hands, a heart holding to its destination. Or is that her, walking back onto the mainland, listening to the curlews calling, or going down into the silver-grey sea and swimming, swimming …?

When seven Welsh bishops called by Tecla's island to pick up a blessing in 603, they received the blessing they wanted not from the hand of Tecla, who was long gone, but at the Pilgrimage Chapel of St Twrog, built above the place where Tecla had her cell. And just like the straggle of people whose curiosity many years before had led them out onto the rock to visit the newly arrived holy woman, the seven bishops were glad to take a blessing where they found one. They needed all the help they could get, because they were on their way to hold a summit meeting at Aust, with Saint Augustine, the very first Archbishop of Canterbury, who the

Pope had sent to speed up the spread of Christianity. The aim of the meeting was nothing less than the reconciliation of the Celtic and Roman branches of the Church, a massive step and one not to be taken lightly if at all. The Welsh bishops had been advised that they should take their cue from the very start of the meeting. If Augustine got to his feet and greeted them as brothers then they should be ready to accept his overtures. If not, they should be fore-warned and prepare to resist. Augustine did not rise to greet them, and the Celtic Church took note, and remained independent … for a little while longer.

The ruins of a chapel still rise from the rock. The tides have taken Tecla's story, though her well still trickles there. Her bones are gone. They are not preserved in any reliquary, except perhaps in the deep treacly silt of the estuary. Mud and silt-filled shells lie along the beach, brought into the light by the ebb tide for a few short hours. It could be that her footprints lie somewhere beneath, showing where she walked away amongst the bivalve shells and the brittle stars.

12

PEGWS

When Pegws spoke or sang in Carmel Chapel in Beaufort, people listened. They sang and they swayed, though she spoke from the pew and not the pulpit. Everyone knew her as Pegws, but her name was Margaret Thomas. When the great Revival had come to North Wales, Pegws was in her teens. In 1804 she heard the Reverend George Lewis speak in her home village of Llangower on the shores of Bala Lake, and she saw people overcome 'as though the wings of the angel of death had touched them' and she was changed forever.

In the years that followed, a young preacher named John Ridge came to minister in Bala and Pegws became a devotee of the man and his works, so much so that when she was forty years old and the Reverend John Ridge left to become pastor at Carmel Chapel, Pegws said farewell to the hills of her birth and walked the hundred miles south to Beaufort on his trail. She became a member of his congregation at Carmel and taught in the Sunday School there. And between Pegws in the pew and the Revered Ridge in the pulpit they say there was a kind of a harmony. In every service his oratory was laced through with her melodious voice, her recitation of texts, her song. And people said of them that 'they acted like oil and fire' and so it was, for many years.

But John Ridge left for Bristol in 1848 and Pegws stayed in Beaufort – and the alchemy of services at Carmel was changed. Visiting ministers came and went and after sitting through one unremarkable sermon Pegws could contain herself no longer. She rose to her feet, recited a verse, linked it to a hymn that she sang loud and sweet, incorporated into the visiting minister's theme and spoke for twenty minutes. The congregation were moved and inspired, the service enlivened, the visiting minister frankly upstaged.

John Ridge's successor at Carmel Chapel was a respected man, the Reverend Thomas Rees. He was a man of method and organisation rather than oil and fire. He planned his sermons thoroughly, and they were well received but they were not, he felt, enhanced by Pegws, who continued to shout out 'Hallelujah' and 'Amen' throughout his delivery. As time went by it all became a bit trying for Thomas Rees and a couple of the wealthier members of the congregation decided to attempt a strategic act of bribery. One morning after the service they took Pegws aside and persuaded her to accept a brand new pair of boots, given to her on the condition that she would restrain herself during the sermon and not disturb the flow of the preacher's oratory. Pegws took the boots. The following week the sermon began and Pegws sat silently in her pew. She managed to maintain that silence until halfway through the sermon, then she got to her feet, pulled off the boots, flung them away down the aisle and shouted, '*Gogoniant i Dduw!* I want Jesus Christ, not your boots!'

Clearly, Pegws was by now oil to her own fire. The deacons, however, expressed their feeling that she was beginning to get senile. Their suspicions seemed to be confirmed when soon afterwards, in response to the Carmel Rebuilding appeal, which was seeking to raise £2,200, Pegws announced a pledge of £5. By now she was seventy-five years old and no one could imagine how she would come by such a sum. But Pegws had already decided she was going to harness the power of a recent discovery – photography. She had brought with her from Bala the traditional Welsh costume she had worn in her younger days, and she knew that people admired it. So she arranged to go to a photographer's studio where she had photographs taken of herself wearing the costume; she then sold souvenir copies for one shilling each and in due course exceeded her £5 target. In the photograph Pegws stands, regarding the viewer with a bright, direct gaze. The chapel was rebuilt in 1865. Pegws lived till she was eighty-eight and her last years were as busy as all the rest had been, gathering wool from the hedges, dyeing it in berry juices, knitting socks and gloves for the poor. Oil to the brightest fire, though she never spoke from the pulpit.

13

BUTTERCUPS

When the young men who came to be called saints wandered through the lands of Gwent, they often spent a good while alone, or with one or two companions or followers. Then as they grew in age and favour, or power or piety or perhaps even wisdom they would settle in a cell, or found a school or monastery. Some of their names were lost along the way, some have come down to us wrapped in the thinnest wisp of story, or not even that. And some of the ones we know most about are the saints who got a 'Life'.

'The Lives of the Saints' are strange, unauthorised biographies written well after their death. 'The Life of Saint Oudoceus' is strange enough on the face of it and investigating a little deeper, from the corner of an eye, suggests a story that is stranger still. Oudoceus is known in Wales as Euddogwy, which seems better suited to the man we find walking by the river.

Euddogwy loved the River Wye and the hills where the streams hurtled down fast and frothy. Perhaps you wouldn't exactly have called him a recluse, but in those early days he certainly didn't seek out company. Slowly but surely his mind and body were growing in tune with the path he had chosen – the path of holiness. He knew that both mind and body needed careful nurturing on that path, and often when he felt in need of that nurturing he went down to the river. He learned a lot by walking beside it. It provided him with instruction, peace of mind and supper.

Early one summer Euddogwy went walking up into the hills. He had set out in the cool of the morning, his feet following an easy rhythm as he climbed; but as the day wore on the sun grew hotter, and though the wooded hills gave shelter from the glare, it was close and muggy. Soon Euddogwy began to get very thirsty. Of course, he knew that the hills were streaked with cool, quick streams and he felt sure it wouldn't be many minutes before he could cup his hands into clear water, quench his thirst and cool his head. But that morning the hillside seemed strangely quiet. There was no sound of falling water, no silvery glints to glimpse between the trees. He reasoned that he had walked further than he usually did, which was true. He was now at the very edges of the lands he knew. But now he was growing thirstier with each step and he was just thinking he would turn and make his way back towards more familiar slopes when all at once he heard two clear sounds together – the splash of water and a woman's laughter.

Euddogwy stopped and listened. He thought now that he could indeed hear the faint sound of a stream a little way ahead and so he pressed on. In a matter of minutes he found himself walking out from beneath the trees towards a pool, neatly terraced into the hillside to catch the outflow of a small spout of water that came bubbling fresh and icy cold from deep within the hill. And thigh-deep in the pool three women were stood washing butter.

Quiet though Euddogwy's approach had been, the women were aware of him at once. Three pairs of eyes turned towards him and, as they gazed silently at him, their hands kept working, dexterously sluicing the sour buttermilk from the golden pats they were forming between their hands. Their sleeves were rolled up to their elbows and their skirts billowed about them in the water. No one spoke. Euddogwy was about to turn and blunder his way back through the trees when one of the women said, 'Be you thirsty?'

Euoddogwy was indeed thirstier than he could say. From the rock the water bubbled busily and loudly into the pool – he couldn't understand how he hadn't heard it from half a mile away. Now he could almost feel it in his throat, and splashing on his hot face. But he could see that there was no vessel, no cup lodged in the rock beside the spout as there usually was, and he had brought no cup tied at his belt as he usually did. And since the women showed no sign of stepping aside he would have to wade past them to get to the spout, past where their skirts floated around their legs, or else cup his hands into the same water where they stood and dipped their arms.

Euddogwy said, 'There is no cup to drink.'

The woman shrugged, but another – Euddogwy at once felt certain it was the one whose laughter he had heard through the trees – smiled and said, 'We have no cup but what is between our hands.'

And all the while the water played between the womens' fingers, washing away the bitter salts. Euddogwy said nothing more, he just turned and made his way quickly back under the shelter of the trees and then he hurried, hurried – not bothering to retrace his steps along the path any more but plunging down in big slithering strides, taking the quickest route to the bottom, tripping on roots, skidding on leaf mould, ducking under branches, barely keeping his feet. On he went, careering down the hill and he didn't stop till he was back down in the valley again where the Wye was flowing as it always did, wide and wise. And there, hot, sweaty and by now desperately thirsty Euddogwy plunged into the water and disappeared entirely beneath the surface for quite a while.

The summer wore on, warm and bright. Euddogwy continued to deepen into the ways of spirit. He would meet a gaze with a steady eye and he spoke clearly, and gently. There was a growing stillness about him; when people met him, they remembered him. And still his life was for the most part a simple and solitary one. One afternoon with the heat of late summer seeming unwilling to give way to autumn, Euddogwy was swimming in the river when a stag came leaping down through the trees. The stag made straight towards the river and when it got to the water's edge it stopped and there, where Euddogwy had left his cloak lying on the bank, the stag collapsed. It lay with its sides heaving as if heart and lungs were about to burst. Seconds later hounds appeared, yelping and sounding as they bounded down the slope on the stag's trail. But when they got to the riverbank where the stag now lay panting for breath on Euddogwy's cloak, the hounds halted. A handful of men on horseback came out of the trees in the wake of the hounds. They too reined in their horses and halted, surveying the scene. And there they were – Euddogwy in the river, the stag stretched out on a cloak, the hounds stopped in their tracks and the mounted men paused behind them.

Out in midstream Euddogwy, who had to keep sculling with his hands so as not to drift off downriver, watched how the hounds stood off in confusion and would not approach the stag where it lay. However hard the huntsmen urged them forward they hung back, forming a little semi-circle several yards from the stag. After a while the hounds lay down and simply looked at the stag. The huntsmen fell silent. Slowly the winded stag began to get its breath back. Still Euddogwy sculled with his arms, keeping his position in the flow of the river, watching the scene unfolding before him on the bank. He saw the stag rise to its feet, take a few hesitant steps and then bound away towards the trees, where it disappeared from view. The hounds got to their feet and watched where the stag went but still they did not move. Only when Euddogwy waded in to shore and picked up his cloak from where it had lain did the hounds start away in full cry – but the huntsmen called them back then, and stayed for a while, speaking with Euddogwy.

And in the weeks and months that followed, the name of Euddogwy and the news of the stag and the cloak began to make its way here and there … to the ears of the Church fathers throughout Gwent and Glamorgan, and to the scattered cottages and clearings on the tree-covered hillsides along the river valley.

One autumn night, when the moon was full and the river lapped high, a woman came walking down from the hill. Silver shadowed from out of the trees she came, with a young child on her hip. Euddogwy recognized her at once. He sat quietly by the riverbank as she approached. When she reached the place where Euddogwy sat she stopped and looked at him, and at his cloak where it lay on the ground at his side.

'Here lies your cloak,' the woman said, and she smiled. 'And the stag upon it still.' And she stretched out her foot and traced a faint outline that could still be seen on the cloth.

He nodded. They both stayed silent for a while, listening to the river murmur.

Then the woman asked, 'Be you thirsty?' and when Euddogwy did not answer she laid her sleeping child quietly on the cloak, and slipped the simple robe she was wearing from her shoulder so that it fell to the ground.

'I have no cup but what is between my hands,' she said. And cupping her hands over her breasts she went down into the river, and Euddogwy followed her. The water and the moonlight enfolded them in silver, and they drifted together downstream, drinking from the night's flow.

Euddogwy never saw the woman again after that night. But once, before autumn gave way to winter, he made his way to the pool high on the hillside terrace. An old grandmother stood there in the water, her hands working the buttermilk from the pats, and a young girlchild stood watching by her side. Euddogwy asked the woman for a little butter, which she gave to him, and he began shaping it into a small rounded cup, bell-shaped, breast-shaped. He stood quietly, holding the small cup between his hands, and it did not melt or lose its form, but grew firmer till at last it sat nestled there on his palm, bright and golden, solid as life. Euddogwy dipped the cup into the water and bowing his head, offered the brimming cupful to the old woman and the child, but they smiled and shook their heads. Euddogwy himself drank then hooked the golden bell-cup onto his belt. He thanked the grandmother, then turned and went on his way. The little child stood watching until he had disappeared between the trees.

Years later, stories spread of the small bright cup that formed itself between the hands of Euddogwy – a miracle from the hands of a miracle-maker. It became a treasured possession of the Church fathers, who guarded it jealously. When they wrote Saint Euddogwy his 'Life', they declared that the miraculous cup was a saintly reprimand to the wickedness and wantonness of women. The cup too was lost, in time. The terraced pool where the women washed butter has crumbled into the earth, swallowed by the roots of the trees that cling to the steep hillside. Down in the valley, the river flows on, wide and wise.

14

PWLL TRA

An owl was flying out low across the ice when she sensed a shift in the air – a change on its way, clear and strong. Below, nothing moved and still the owl flew on, cleaving the air silently, her head turning a little this way and that. She was readying herself to see from which direction change would come. She was readying herself to recognise a new world. Then a deep shudder cracked open the white face of the land; a mass of ice cascaded, fell away. The land shrugged and settled again. The air was thick with fine, cold crystals. The owl's bright flight disappeared from view across the horizon of the years.

On a chilly morning in late autumn a thin man, poorly dressed and nipped with cold, stumbled along Mynydd Henllys towards a house that stood with its face blank and its large sturdy door firmly closed, keeping its warmth close to its chest. Apart from the thin man picking his way slowly onwards, nothing moved. The man knew the house, or had known of it all his life. His mother had described it to him, saying that she had once lived there. She was a daughter of the house, she told him – only her foot had stumbled on the path that had been set out for her. She had been sent away then, hardly even a grown girl. His mother was long-gone now and there was no more family. Only his wife, who was lying too sick and weak to move on the hill, by the stones of a ruined sheepcote that gave very little shelter.

The thin man knocked on the door of the house he had known about for so long. As he stood waiting, the wind began to blow around the house, and its fingers quickly found their way through his ragged coat to his ribs and probed there without asking permission. From inside the house a scent began to rise and the scent found its way under the door and into the thin man's nostrils. It was the smell of mutton and mint and fine-grease gravy. It was Dinner. The man knocked again and waited again. The wind went on exploring inside his coat and the smell of Dinner went on caressing the inside of his nostrils. The man knocked at the door for a third time and at last he heard small steps hurrying, then the door was opened by a young maid who looked at the thin man and said nothing. He told her he was desperately in want of a crust and a drink of broth for his wife who was sick and hungry. The maid carried on saying nothing at all for another moment or so then she disappeared back inside the house, leaving the door just half an inch ajar and the thin man still stood on the outside of it. After a while there was a rustle of heavy skirts and the lady of the house appeared in the doorway. She too looked at the thin man without saying anything and the thin man repeated to the lady of the house what he had already said to the maid, because he didn't have anything else to say.

The woman's mouth was close and tight as a scar. Her fingers were clamped soundly around the head of a walking stick and she kept the stick tap-tap-tapping on the ground all the time the man was speaking. Then the thin man fell silent, swaying with exhaustion where he stood. The scent of roast mutton and mint and fine-grease gravy wrapped itself more strongly around his senses, around the tapping stick, around the world.

Then the woman said, 'I know your look. I don't care who your mother was. I've got food a-plenty; my kitchen is well stocked and no one under my roof who works hard and is honest goes hungry. But I have nothing for those who go creeping and skulking about like wretches, like whining creatures of no worth. So you may get along home and do not come looking at this house again for generosity, which I plainly see you do not deserve.'

The instant the woman of the house had finished this speech she signalled to the maid and turned away, disappearing back inside the house. The thin man pulled his coat tighter around him and said wearily, 'And if we are all to get what we deserve, how will we fare?'

But the door closed on his words. And then there was little the man could do other than turn and make his weary way back towards the hillside, to where his wife lay waiting in the lee of a tumble of stones. But he hadn't gone far when there was shift and a shudder beneath him, above him, around him, and as he struggled to stay on his feet on the quaking land he saw that away behind him, the house with its blank face and its closed door and its mutton and its mint and its fine-grease gravy was sinking down, being swallowed up by the ground.

In the hollow where the house once stood there is now a pool of water, though shrinking back in summer heat, it never fully drains away. It is called *Pwll Tra* – the Pool of Avarice.

One hot summer day as I walked to the pool, knowing it would be bright with the dragonflies and damselflies that love it, a tawny owl overtook me, flying in low over the foxgloves, as if she were on her way to listen for voices beneath the water, or trying to sense from which direction change would come.

15

Spirit Margaret

There was once a woman named Margaret Richard who rose early to her chores, carried milk to the house and worked every day until sunset. She was expecting a child. The father of the child was a man named Samuel Richard, and he and Margaret were due to be married. So far, nothing unusual. On the day appointed for the marriage, Margaret arrived at the little grey church of St Mary's Panteg, with a couple of friends for company and to act as witnesses. They waited and they waited, but Samuel Richard did not arrive. The blood in Margaret's face and neck rose up red as she stood waiting by the altar but as the minutes ticked by and there was still no sign of Samuel, Margaret's face paled to a sickly white. When the rector and the witnesses said they could wait no longer, Margaret Richard went down on her knees and said a short simple prayer, into which she poured every ounce of presence of mind and consciousness intention that she could muster.

'I pray to Almighty God,' said Margaret, 'that Samuel Richard will have no rest in this world or the next.' Then she got to her feet and the solemn little group left the church.

Soon afterwards, it happened that Samuel Richard fell ill and died. Margaret continued much as she had before, rising early to her chores, carrying milk to the house – and nurturing the child that was growing in her belly. But almost immediately after Samuel's death, he began to come to Margaret in spirit form, and this was a great trouble to her. However loath Samuel had been to put in an appearance as a bridegroom, he now started to turn up with great regularity. Not so often in the daytime, but as the sun began to set and until it rose again Margaret could see him almost all the time, just in the corner of her eye. And if she could not *see* him, she knew he was there: in the ray of moonlight coming in through the dusty kitchen window, in the whispering leaves of the beech trees along the hollow lane, there he was.

Whenever Samuel appeared there was a restlessness about him. He was never still or quiet, there was always a rustling and a muttering and Margaret got into the habit of calling out 'Be quiet!' or 'Go away!' or 'Leave me alone!' and she would go out into the yard and clatter pans loudly in the darkness, or break into a run if she was making her way home along the hollow lane. But however much she hurried or busied herself and however much of a clatter and a commotion she made, still he would come, and she would know at once that he was there. She told everyone about it and no one was really in any doubt. They could see it in her face. It was disturbing but clearly it was true that Margaret Richard was now being haunted by Samuel Richard. And soon, while she was still heavy with the child, people began to refer to her as *Margaret yr Ysbryd* – Spirit Margaret.

And Spirit Margaret rose early to her chores, just the same as plain old Margaret had done. She carried milk to the house, she worked each day until sunset. And now she kept house not so much 'amongst a cloud of witnesses', as the saying goes, but in the uneasy knowledge that Samuel Richard was never far away, and that he would draw closer still with the onset of dusk. The knowledge seeped into every moment, waited at every corner. She began to feel lightheaded, but not pleasantly so, and even her simple everyday activities took on a tinge of otherworldliness because she was so alert to the realm of spirit and the presence of the departed Samuel. When Margaret carried the milk back to the house now, she felt vague and faint, and it was all she could do to lift the pail up to fill the jug on the table. And when she did, even if it tilted and tipped between her hands as she struggled, *the milk never spilled from the jug*. In fact, the milk never splashed or moved at all, but stayed still and settled as she poured it. Numerous people saw this and shook their heads in concern, taking it as another clear indication that a haunting spirit was at work.

Spirit Margaret grew paler and more unquiet in her mind with each day that passed. At last, when delivering a pail of milk to the house of Mr Hercules Jenkins at Trostre, she felt so faint that she actually tipped the jug right over after she had filled it *and still not a single drop of milk spilled out*. Then she covered her face with her hands and she wept. At that point Mrs Hercules Jenkins, who had observed the whole thing, set the jug right way up again and sat Spirit Margaret down on the settle, where she cried and cried over the not-spilt milk. Then the solid and quietly spoken Mrs Hercules Jenkins made them both a cup of tea and she sat down beside Spirit Margaret and patted her hand gently and gave the following advice:

'My dear,' she said, once Spirit Margaret's sobs had lessened a little, 'should you chance to meet with this person now on your way home, speak to him. Ask him what he wants from you, and if you can, tell him that you forgive him. And then perhaps things will become a little clearer.'

'It is without any doubt that I will meet with him,' said Spirit Margaret wearily, 'because it's already getting dark.'

She set off home as soon as she was able, and sure enough she hadn't gone farther than the little footbridge over the stream that ran past Mrs Hercules Jenkins' vegetable garden when she saw Samuel. He was sat there on the stile. She could not pass over the bridge without speaking to him, and so she took the advice she had been given. Forcing herself to look straight at Samuel she asked, 'What do you want with me, Samuel?'

The reply came clear and steady, in the voice she remembered very well.

'I want nothing except that you forgive me, then I will never trouble you any more.'

And Spirit Margaret forgave Samuel Richard. He reached towards her and they shook hands in a friendly way. Almost at once, she felt his grip dwindle and dissolve away beneath her fingers. Then he was no longer sat on the stile, and she passed on over the little footbridge and made her way home.

16

CONJURING AT HOME

There was a man who lived in Devauden and he was a conjuror. His wife, although she came to it a little reluctantly, assisted him as best she could. Soon after they married, he had produced a little blue jewel from behind her ear, and she was startled and hadn't really known what to do. When he suggested that she might like to put the jewel on a chain around her neck, she thought for a moment, then she hung it in the window, where it split the light into a thousand little rainbow-fish that danced on the walls and ceiling. The conjuror was what is sometimes called 'a man of his square mile' and he did most of his conjuring at home, or in the immediate locality. He was a quiet, pleasant man, well-liked by his neighbours. His wife was well thought of too, especially by the other women, who often commented to one another that all things considered it was probably a mixed blessing to have a conjuror for a husband.

As time went on the conjuror of Devauden grew more and more skilled at his craft. And he became a little more inventive and just a little bolder too, though still in a quiet, homely way. One morning his wife got up and discovered with a shock that there was a small oak tree growing in the middle of the kitchen. It was pushing its way sturdily up through the floor, there where her husband had conjured it, and though it wasn't much more than a sapling it was in full leaf and with a generous crop of green acorns growing. She made herself a cup of tea with two spoonfuls of sugar (for the shock) and sat down to drink it. By the time she had finished she was sure the little oak tree had already grown a couple more inches. It was a magical thing, that much was certain. If it kept on growing, she would have to edge around it just to get to the range, she thought. And the neighbours would be in and out to see it all day long.

She was correct on all points. The oak tree in the floor did keep on growing, and the neighbours were in and out to see it – but not just the neighbours. Rumours of the tree spread, and folks began traipsing over from Raglan and Usk and Monmouth to have a look. She didn't quite know what to say to her husband about this, because he was proud of his achievements, and so was she, really, despite the inconvenience. As a couple, they had not really mastered the art of truly communicative conversation, and so niggling concerns were not easily aired.

Before long, the oak tree began to drop copious amounts of ripening acorns onto the kitchen floor, where they got underfoot and made you skid and turn your ankle. At that point, the conjuror must have sensed that there might be a few difficulties that needed addressing. One afternoon when his wife came in from hanging out the washing, she found a sow and a litter of delighted, squealing piglets rootling across the kitchen floor, gobbling up the fallen acorns – and clattering into pans and crockery and spreading muck as they did so. The conjuror came in from the further room for a moment as his wife stood surveying the scene. In those days people didn't say 'Da-daaa!' when they'd performed a clever act, but instead the conjuror nodded in a satisfied and pleased sort of way. He smiled brightly at his wife. Her face went bright red and she bit her lip. The conjuror withdrew in some confusion. When he had gone, the woman looked long and hard at the sow, who turned her small twinkly eyes upon her and returned her gaze. Several volumes of understanding passed between them.

The woman turned on her heels and walked out of the kitchen. The sow trotted beside her and all eleven little piglets scampered along behind as fast as their podgy, acorn-filled bellies would allow. The woman strode across several fields and on up the hillside, and she did not stop until she got to the hilltop. There she sat down, her back leaning against the sow. The piglets flopped down all around, and were asleep and snoring within seconds.

She sat there for a good long time looking out over the valley, where her own little house nestled. She thought about magic. About husbands. About how the world is and how much there was to know and guess at and explore. The land spread away below her. It was a fine view, with the little streams and lanes all heading off in so many different directions. She was wearing good, sturdy shoes for walking, too.

She sat on the hill all day, till the light began to fade. As the sun's rays began to turn the sky pink, she glanced at her own little house down in the valley just in time to see a flight of multicoloured birds fly up out of the chimney.

17

THE SECRET OF THE OLD JAPAN HOUSE

Iron veins and coal bones lie rich and strong beneath the green skin of the Eastern Valley. When the ironmasters arrived and the workers came in their thousands, the valley was the centre of the world. Iron veins, coal bones and fast-flowing, stone-breaker rivers – and trees, trees, trees to burn.

The town of Pontypool grew up in the midst of it all – not too noticeably at first, when the blacksmiths worked their iron with charcoal heat and hand bellows; but as soon as there were blast furnaces and waterwheels and gigantic bellows, little hamlets like Trosnant and Pontymoel began to merge and flow together in the sheer frenzied heat of it all. The Hanbury family of bankers from London came and settled themselves, intent on cornering the market in the production of higher-grade Osmond iron. As their dynasty grew and the ironworks grew, the town of Pontypool appeared and consolidated.

Amongst the flow of skilled and unskilled workers who began arriving from near and far towards the end of the seventeenth century came Thomas Allgood, a Quaker from Northamptonshire, and his little family. Thomas was a diligent and resourceful man and he was set to work on one of the most pressing challenges of the time, which was tinplating. In a time before plastic, coating iron sheets with a thin protective layer of tin could enable the making of all kinds of handy objects if only it could be done efficiently and reliably. Under Thomas Allgood's direction, the challenge was tackled head-on. Before long the Pontypool works became the first in Britain to carry out tinplating on a commercial scale and Thomas's own son, Edward, became works manager.

Now, there is no doubt that the tinplate Thomas Allgood produced was hugely useful and practical, but Edward was a man with a leaning towards the decorative. He was especially intrigued by the oriental art of lacquering, where wooden objects were shaved so fine that the light shone through, then varnished to produce the most exquisite objects and pieces of furniture. And Edward reasoned that if oriental cabinetmakers could use wood in this way, Welsh tinplate makers might just be able to do something similar, if not better. So, building on the techniques his father had devised, Edward began to experiment to see if he could find a way of giving tinplate a similar brilliant, decorative finish. If he succeeded, the many useful objects they were manufacturing could be beautiful as well as useful – and also sell for more money.

Edward kept his eyes and ears open, and went in search of clues as and when he could. He had already grasped the useful life lesson that when you play dumb and ask friendly questions, people sometimes tell you things they otherwise wouldn't. Armed with this strategy Edward went to the renowned ironworks at Woburn and played the part of the harmless and impressionable idiot who knows just enough to ask a few questions. It seems the strategy worked, because Edward was allowed to watch and listen. And that was all he needed. He soaked up all kinds of tips and hints and made connections in his mind, and before long he was back in Pontypool setting up a brand new business with his brothers and producing a brand new thing. It was a thing that nobody knew they needed until they heard about it, but when they did, everybody wanted it. It was a thing they called *Japanware*; real oriental style, made in a cottage in Trosnant.

The secret of it all lay in the lacquer. In the Orient, the lacquer had always come from the Varnish Tree. It was tapped like rubber, by making diagonal cuts in the bark of the tree and collecting the flowing sap in a cup. In one season a mature tree would yield about half a cup of milky white liquid that turned black on contact with the air. This substance was so poisonous that even the fumes were dangerous to inhale. Varnish Tree workers had to build up immunity to the poison by the make-or-break process of gradually increased exposure. Now, the forests of the Eastern Valley of Monmouthshire had been extensive, lush and magical places where many different trees species grew – although these forests had shrunk rapidly with the coming of industry. But even in their pre-industrial glory these forests had not been home to Varnish Trees. So, to make his genuine oriental tinplate coating, Edward Allgood had to come up with a substitute. Which he did. I can't tell you exactly what it was, because in a way nobody can. I can only say that the ingredients lay for the most part in the veins and bones of the land, because that's where Edward looked for them. Shale oils and iron ores and something else besides, something secret …

It was soon clear that Edward and his brothers had come up with a winner. The black-lacquered goods they produced, with their shiny golds and blues and browns and red-coloured designs, were a huge success. The little cottage in Trosnant – already known locally as the Old Japan House – was selling all it could produce. Landed gentry ordered bespoke items with picturesque views of their country estates painted brightly on them. Humble, practical domestic items of all kinds were made into little objects of desire – candlesticks, teapots, trays and snuffboxes, not cheap, but a delight to behold. In 1755, a visitor to the area noted with some astonishment that 'an ordinary butter dish with a yellow rose painted on it sells for two shillings'.

And the method of manufacture, and the ingredients used in the varnish, well, that remained the secret of the Allgood family, and they held it close all down the years.

But families are made up of people and the thing about people is that they're not always very good at holding secrets close for long periods of time. Especially when they quarrel, which is exactly what the Allgood grandsons did. The upshot of the quarrel was that two of them went off to set up a rival japanware-producing hub in Usk. Both factions advertised prolifically in the local newspapers, each claiming to be the guardians of the original secret of the production of the now famous Pontypool Ware. In those days, secrets were in some respects easier to guard. For one thing, any apprentices brought in to the japanworks were sworn to secrecy – they were bound to the mystery, as were apprentices in other trades, with a seven-year indenture. They probably didn't have much inclination to gossip anyway, since they worked a minimum sixty-hour week in gruelling and exhausting conditions, which probably tended to limit the opportunities for careless chatter. But apprentices who lasted the course would eventually be free to spread their wings at some point, or take their skills elsewhere. And it wasn't long before the growing manufacturing centres of Birmingham, Wolverhampton and Bilston had sent their own scouts to Pontypool, talent-poaching and maybe indulging in a bit of industrial espionage, much as Edward the elder had done himself on his visit to Woburn. And they were soon back off home and producing 'Pontypool Ware' themselves. And they were producing it more cheaply, and in bigger quantities.

Meanwhile, in Pontypool and Usk, the two factions of the Allgood family were working hard to maintain the mystique of their original recipe as produced in the Old Japan House. By now there was scarcely time to make bespoke pieces for the gentry because the struggle was on to keep up with the flow of japanware coming from the Midlands. But the Allgoods were by no means finished. Cometh the hour, cometh the man – in this case, the Bagman: William Allgood, the several-times-great-grandson of Thomas, known as Billy the Bagman because of his extraordinary salesman's energy and enthusiasm. Billy was proud of his family's goods and he rolled up his sleeves and got on with the job of promoting them, loud and clear, at home and abroad. And he put his money where his mouth was. One time Billy was sat in the Red Lion in Albion Street when a salesman from one of the Midlands works dared to suggest that his wares were better – a dangerous boast on Billy's home ground. Billy stood a £5 wager and they both produced snuffboxes that, when examined by customers, were declared to be of equal quality. Billy then said, 'Now let's see what real Pontypool Japan is!' and threw his snuffbox into the fire. The man from the Midlands would not follow suit. Billy then removed his snuffbox completely unscathed from the flames and claimed his winnings.

Billy the Bagman died on a selling trip to London and with the death of that salesman, the end was in sight. Billy's daughter Mary had worked as a painter of flowers and peacocks on trays and when she died in 1848 the Pontypool secret was deemed to be lost. Nor had the Reverend Lewis Usk Jones, who had inherited the Usk business, ever divulged details. The commercial mystique that the Allgood family had managed to maintain continued on after their days. Then in 1875 a local newspaper, the *Usk Gleaner*, had some exciting news concerning japanware:

> The mighty secret is not irretrievably lost! Mr Bythway, solicitor of Pontypool still holds it … and he is willing to treat with any gentleman who may desire to revive the manufacture.

But no gentleman did so desire, and another half century passed by before the *Free Press* of Monmouthshire made a dramatic announcement:

Recipe for Pontypool Japan ware found in Ancient Diary.

The 'Ancient Diary' was in fact the diary that had belonged to Mr Bythway, solicitor of Pontypool, and had been discovered at the back of his desk by his son Mr W. Bythway. The *Free Press* declared itself full of wild hope:

Although we have no authentic information of any steps which may follow the romantic discovery, its possibility in the realms of both art and science is boundless and we shall await with the deepest interest the sequels which we feel sure it is bound to have.

But nothing more was revealed or published. Boundless possibility remained just that, and before his death in 1949, Mr W. Bythway gave the document to the care of the National Museum.

In more recent years, call-outs for information have sent various manufacturers rummaging through old bills of supply, piecing together details of methods and quantities, temperatures, shades and techniques for the original clear and black varnish, the characteristic tortoiseshell finish, the rare blue colour. Now we have reliable details of layering six to eight coats of varnish, each four thousandth of an inch thick; of local iron ores that give crimsons, vermilions and browns; of linseed oil both raw and boiled, of walnut and poppyseed. We see the lists of pigments, gums and resins with marvellous names – smalt and orpiment, lamp black and umber, copal, dragons' blood, Venice turpentine and isinglass. With all this, we can put together a fairly accurate picture of the production process.

But we do not have the secret of the Old Japan House. Nor would Mr Bythway's 'Ancient Diary' have related to the original formulation, but to the declining years at Usk, by which time processes had already changed. But even if it had, it would not have been *the secret*. Because that lies in the sudden flare of beauty and timely inventiveness; it lies in the moment of inspiration meeting patient, hard work. New materials and methods arise, yesterday's pigments and oils and finishes become obsolete. But the bright, illuminating, life-enhancing flare of inspiration does not. We yearn for it, like a precious thing we can never quite believe is lost. We yearn for the secret behind the secret.

18

MALLT Y NÔS

There is a woman who rides with a man though the air, some nights. Dogs bound beside them, and the dogs are *Cwn Annwn*; the Otherworld hounds, the skydogs. You can tell because they are white with red ears. They run wildest in the long, stormy wide-awake nights of winter. It is the Lord of the Otherworld who rides with them, and it is the woman of many names who is at his side, and one of her names is Mallt y nôs. This is the story of how Mallt came to ride with the Wild Hunt over the hills of Gwent.

Mallt was once a woman of flesh, blood and spirit. She was clever and decisive and a little bit impetuous. When she was a girl what she loved most of all was running, running as fast as her legs would carry her, and riding. And when she rode it was not at a canter but at full gallop. A few of the girls she grew up with were just the same, but as they grew older, they seemed to Mallt to ride just a little bit more sedately (though most of them denied it), and when they settled into life as wives and mothers quite a few of them hardly did any running at all – unless they had to make a sudden dash to stop a toddler falling into the stream. If anything, Mallt rode harder and faster as she grew into womanhood and she couldn't imagine that anything would ever get in the way of that.

In due course, Mallt also married. In fact, she married well; that is, she married a fairly good-natured man with money and a small castle. He liked to laugh, he was a good lover and he was away a lot, all excellent qualities. He had several good horses and he and Mallt rode out every day, alone or with the hunting parties. There Mallt was in her element and the joy and sheer thrill of riding with the hunters made her most alive, most in tune with the world. People even claimed to have heard her say that if there were no good horses in heaven, then she didn't want to go there. And all was well and good, except for one small thing.

Mallt's husband had given her an instruction – only one – which really rankled. He told her that when he was away she should not ride out with the hunting parties, but keep within the home acre. Mallt argued against this loud and long but her husband took no notice and eventually she shut up. But inwardly, and out loud when she thought there was no one around to hear her, Mallt howled with frustration. It was worst when she saw the hunters pass by, and she watched the hawks rising bright into the sky and she heard the hooves of the fine horses thudding over the hillside. Then, however hard she tried to busy herself with something else, she could feel her heart pounding in her chest and the blood rising in her face because she was not riding with them, and the wind was not in her hair and the hawk was not rising from her hand.

Early one morning when her husband was away, Mallt was riding in the meadows of her home acre when she heard the sound of a horn on the breeze. She turned her horse's head to the sound and in an instant they were off, not at a canter but at full gallop. Away and over the hills, far from the home acre. And Mallt rode all day with the hunters until every drop of blood in her veins sang for joy of this wild life, and the wild hills and skies. And as evening came she turned for home, safe in the knowledge that her husband would not return till the following day.

But Mallt was mistaken. Her husband's business had concluded early and he was stood waiting for her in the bailey. When he saw her ride in, her horse a little lame from the day's hunting, he strode across and angrily took hold of the bridle. As Mallt began to dismount he grabbed her arm and somehow or other she landed heavily on her ankle, which slipped from beneath her and twisted and cracked and Mallt shrieked out sharply with the sudden shock of pain. And nobody who was watching that night or who heard the shriek would speak willingly of what happened next. And those who did speak gave different accounts, saying that when he bent to pick her up from the ground she twisted in his arms, or that he struck her but she dodged the blow ... they fought or they embraced ... they shouted or they grappled in silence.

But the one thing that all agree on is that all of a sudden a wind began to gust and Mallt's hair began to stream into that wind. Her stained robes fluttered and flapped wildly like flags around her until she was carried bodily upwards, one hand torn from the grip of her husband's fist as she was lifted into the swirling sky. But her other hand stayed twisted tight around her horse's rein and as Mallt rose the horse too was taken up in that whirlwind and in the distance a howling pack of hounds raced across the sky on that wind and came surging around them. The head of that Wild Hunt shouted out as Mallt and her horse blew up to his side. Then Mallt and the huntsman – who was none other than Arawn, the Lord of the Otherworld himself – rode off into the wild night, off across the windswept hills of Gwent and far beyond. And they ride together still.

19

BLACK, WHITE AND GREY

On the hills of south-east Wales there are women moving, some are old and some are older. They are shaded white, grey, black and may be seen in different circumstances. You may see the Old Woman of the Mountain, you may see Gwrach y rhibyn, you may see Ladi Wen. Most likely you will simply see mist settling around the shoulder of the hill like a shawl. The thought might worry you.

In fact, you might decide that you would rather not walk on the hills at all – except that sometimes there is no choice. The hill path must be taken, the mountain must be crossed. And you may be born on those hills and know them like the back of your hand, but the old women who are out walking these hills are mistresses of misdirection. Within a quarter of a mile of setting out, the landscape you grew up in is changed to something unknown and unknowable. Now your views are not of home but of nowhere.

If that happened to you now, you would probably stop and get your phone out to check your location – but are you sure there would be a signal? So you may say to yourself, 'Alright, it's just a bit of hill fog, I'll wait for a gap in the mist, I'll get my compass out, I'll look at the map, I'll get my bearings. Worst comes to the worst, I'll sit it out. Come on, I got my Duke of Edinburgh Bronze Medal, didn't I?' And you may do all those things; but if you are having an encounter with the Old Woman of the Mountain, for example, then your strategies would be in vain (even if you had your Duke of Edinburgh *Gold* Medal). To begin with, there might be a kind of whooping sound, and somewhere in front of you a shape you almost recognised would stretch out a hand and beckon you. Come on, this way … And you would follow, because in most of us there is something that will follow, and the call would come again and again, sometimes seeming to come from near at hand, sometimes far in the distance. You would follow, and not until the mist drifted away after what seemed like an eternity would you observe that you had ended up exactly where you began. At that point your signal would probably return, or at least three bars.

And so, despite your best efforts and the benefits of modern technology, you would have become part of a story that really is as old as the hills. What just happened to you wouldn't really be much different to what happened to John ap John when he set out before daylight to walk to Caerleon Fair, although that was a long time ago now. On Milfre Mountain John heard a voice calling from Bryn Mawr, then from Bwlch y llyn, then Gilfach fields. Near and far, but the same voice; he knew the Old Woman of the Mountain did this very thing, he'd grown up knowing it. And he began to follow – even though he knew the way, even though he had no need whatsoever to follow, and the light began to dawn so misty, so hazy. It was the between time, the time when people get stolen away from the places they know like the back of their hand. Then when he heard coach wheels, and the voice was still calling, he flung himself on the grass, which was damp from the foggy grey dawn that was breaking. John ap John did not want to get stolen away from what he knew. He summoned all his resolve and he screwed his eyes tight shut. When he opened them, the sun had risen, the birds were singing, and best of all, sheep were grazing; real, solid, ordinary sheep. And there was still plenty of time to get to Caerleon Fair.

Yes, on the mountains of south-east Wales there are women moving. They are shaded black, white and grey and may be seen in different circumstances. Perhaps they are there because the mountains are there, or perhaps it's the other way around. They can appear solid as rock or as insubstantial as hill mist. Look, there is Gwrach y Rhibyn in her misty form, with droplets of damp fog in her hair and a shroud for a gown. And into that pale and tattered gown she has gathered many names, and amongst them are the names of old women who lived alone on the hillside, whole generations of them, whole families, most of us have forgotten them now, though she has not.

On Mynydd Llanhiledd at one time they gave a new a name to the old woman they heard calling in the mist. They said her name was Juan White. But Juan White – or Siwan Gwyn – had been a woman of more than old bones and a twist of fog. She had lived alone for a long while in a cottage on the Lasgarn Hill near Pontypool, where some people called on her when they were in need of help and some people chose to give her a wide berth. When she died, whether it was of her choosing or not, her shroud was swapped for a damp cloak of hill fog that was twisted around her shoulders. And now they said it was Juan White who was there, calling out for you to follow her. You could tell because she wore a four-cornered hat, just like she always had, with ash-coloured clothes, and a wooden pail in her hand to carry milk. She called

'*Wowwwwwwwup!*' through the mist – sometimes close by, some-times away over on the other side of the mountain in Aberystruth. And everybody swore the hill was never haunted till Juan White died. But they had forgotten that the Old Woman of the Mountain has been walking, walking on the hills for the longest time.

Sometimes, the mist through which these old ones move will drift and thin to clear, bright sunlight; sometimes Gwrach y Rhibyn's shroud falls away to reveal a blackness beneath. Then the blackness clots, becomes more solid, and dark leathery skin takes form as she flies low along the streams, tattered gown flap-flapping. Then she is bat-wing black, limbs shrunk, eyes sunk deep and piercing. She makes fly-bys at the bedroom windows of old houses and the sight and sound of her is taken as foreshadowing a death. So the people of Gwent would say, 'It's only the old stock she troubles.' The old stock, who remembered many things, not the newcomers who came with different stories.

But stories will change and change again in ways we don't foresee. And Gwrach y Rhibyn enfolds black within white so that it shades again into the shifting grey fog. Ghost white of mothwing to crow-feather black on the mountain, even today. Even if you're certain that you know your way.

TEN

When Albinia Beatrix Wherry, 'Bea' to her friends, spent the summer in Penallt, she was all set to collect stories. Maybe ones about wise men and ghosts, she thought. And resourceful women. Her plan was to sit quietly and listen attentively. She would make notes and nod encouragingly to the tellers, and with luck she might collect some tales worth remembering. It was a good plan, though not all tellers and not all tales will let you sit quietly and nod encouragement from the sidelines. Some will insist on taking your hand and pulling you close – and when it is done it may be the telling you remember as vividly as the tale itself.

One afternoon, Granny England (or Mrs Briton, as Bea called her), took her arm companionably and announced that the time had come to go to Trellech to call on old Mrs Pryce, who she felt would be quite happy to come and share a story or two.

'Particularly as I've made tea and bara brith,' said Mrs Briton. 'Because at present Mrs Pryce is sorely vexed by the rent being due, and there is some debate as to how she might be able to pay it.'

So they set off arm-in-arm down the warm leafy lanes to Trellech. When they arrived, they found Mrs Pryce standing in the yard. She was wearing a heavy all-weather cloak despite the sunshine, and she was surrounded by most of her remaining possessions, which she was trying to sell. As soon as she set eyes on them Mrs Pryce waved aside introductions and peered brightly at Bea from under her bonnet.

'Now, will you have need of a fine oak table?' she asked. 'Or a few of these good chairs? I don't have need of them any longer, since I do live alone. I can easily make do with the old bench I used to kill pigs on. 'Twill not be used for that again,' she said, 'so I may as well sit on it as long as I do live.'

Bea wasn't in need of a table or chairs but she felt sure that there was a story already drawing her in. Full of anticipation, she sailed back along the lanes tucked between Mrs Briton and Mrs Pryce – who seemed happy to leave her chairs and worldly goods sunning themselves in the yard while they made their way back to the tea and bara brith.

The tale that Mrs Pryce and Mrs Briton decided should be told concerned a man named Old Jenkyns. Bea had already heard quite a bit about Old Jenkyns, because he had been a conjuror, and things had happened when he was about, and he was a Fount of Knowledge, and so naturally his views and opinions found their way into many things.

'One day,' Mrs Pryce began, 'Old Jenkyns was going to town and he was on his way down towards Grosmont when he felt the need of refreshment and he stopped at the Cock and Feather. He sat himself down at the table – a fine oak table it was too – and asked the landlady for bread and cheese and beer, which she provided, and filled the pint very nicely. When he was thoroughly refreshed and ready to continue on his way, Old Jenkyns asked how much he owed.'

'Now …' said Mrs Briton.

'Now …' said Mrs Pryce.

There was a pause. Bea sat up a little straighter in her chair, and a little more alert. Mrs Pryce continued:

'"Let's see," says the landlady. "Six and four is ten … so that will be ten pence please." And Old Jenkyns sits for a while but he never says a word. He just gives her a look. She might have thought something about that look, but she didn't. Old Jenkyns pays her the ten pence, then he goes on his way, and she follows after him, politely seeing him to the door.'

'Now…' said Mrs Briton.

'Now…' said Mrs Pryce.

Bea began to fidget a little and her shoes tapped on the floor once or twice. Mrs Briton and Mrs Pryce were soon explaining how, when the landlady came back into the kitchen to clear away the things from the table where Old Jenkyns had been sitting, she immediately began to jiggle.

'It was her legs started,' said Mrs Pryce.

'Then all the rest of her,' said Mrs Briton.

'And off she goes running round and round that table, it was a fine big one, solid oak, and every time she gets to the place where Jenkyns had been sat with his bread and cheese and his beer she calls out:

> *Six and four is ten*
> *Here's off again!'*

And Mrs Briton ran around the table, and Mrs Pryce, still wrapped in her heavy cloak although the kitchen was full of sunshine, peered from her bonnet, eyes bright and penetrating.

'*Six and four is ten!*' she said, tapping her foot.

'*Six and four is ten!*' and round and round the table Mrs Briton ran ... and Bea couldn't help but get to her feet ...

'Now then,' continued one or other of the women, Bea wasn't quite sure which one because she was concentrating on not bumping into the table. 'Presently, the landlady's daughter, who is sixteen years of age, hears the commotion and she pops her head around the door and sees her mother running round and around the table and calling out:

> *Six and four is ten*
> *Here's off again!*'

The daughter leans against the doorpost and watches this spectacle with interest. She thinks she should probably go and catch hold of her mother's arm and sit her down, since she didn't seem able to stop of her own accord. But outside the sun was on the hill and the hay in the meadow was golden and smelling like magic. And the daughter slips away quietly and off she goes to lie in the meadow, alone or not as the case might be ...'

'Now ...' said Mrs Pryce.

'Now ...' puffed Mrs Briton, still running.

'Now ...' thought Bea, still following.

'The landlady goes on running around and around that big old oak table, and every time she passes the chair where Jenkyns had sat she calls out:

> *Six and four is ten*
> *Here's off again!*'

'And on she runs for an hour and a half. And round about then her son comes back from work, and he looks around the door and he says, "What's the matter mother?"

'And she looks at him pitifully but she keeps on running, though now her poor chest is heaving and her legs can scarcely carry her and she waves her hands and she gasps, "I don't know!"

'So he stands watching her for a while, wondering. Then he goes to the back door and there was his sister coming back from the meadow with a wisp of hay in her hair and he says, "Has Old Jenkyns been around this way today?" And his sister says, "I think he might have been, I can't say, I've been so busy."

'And the boy goes off down the road, ever such a long way, and at last he sees Old Jenkyns sat by the roadside giving his opinion to a group of old codgers there. And he goes up and he tells Jenkyns that his mother is running round and round the table and breathing fit to burst. So Jenkyns says, "Serves her right for charging an honest man ten pence for a bit of bread and cheese and a sip of beer!" and he carries on finishing what he was saying to the old codgers. And the boy stays there, stubborn, and at last Jenkyns says to him, "You go back to your kitchen now and look under the old candlestick on the shelf above the fireplace. There's a bit of paper under it. You don't look at the paper, or it'll be the worse for you, but you throw that paper on the fire and it's all done with, and it must be hoped she will have learned her lesson."

'And the boy goes off home and there is his mother —'

'Six and four is ten …' gasped Mrs Briton, her belly wobbling, her sides heaving, her skirts trembling, and she and Bea leaning into one another to stop themselves from falling

'— there is his mother, still running around the table. And he goes and looks under the candlestick and there is the bit of paper as Old Jenkyns had said, and the lad throws it on the fire quick. AND DOWN SHE GOES!' concluded Mrs Pryce.

'And her old chest going like a bellows!' added Mrs Briton.

And then and there she and Mrs Pryce and Albinia Beatrix Wherry collapsed in a heap.

And they sat there for a while on the settle, all three of them, the sun pouring in through the window, shaking and laughing and nodding, and then they finished up the last few crumbs of bara brith and went out into the summer afternoon, and back down the lane, to see if anyone had come for Mrs Pryce's chairs yet.

21

CLEAN AND CLEVER

It is well known that if you dance with the fairy folk you're asking for trouble. Or even if you don't actually dance with the fairy folk but just dance by yourself in a fairy ring at twilight or possibly at sunrise, or by a certain tree at midsummer or on a May morning. There are some times and places when you just dance at your own risk and that's that. It probably won't end well; you'll dance for a few moments and then turn round to find that the whole land-scape has changed and everyone you know has died and the pub has closed and the internet has been invented. Or perhaps you keep on dancing, and never come back to the world at all. Of course, the fairy folk are the best dance partners. Lilt to the music with them and you are a deer in the spring forest, a fine ship on a high sea – you move as one with the moving spirit of the world and it is delightful. I think it must be like that. But however much of a delight it is, you are supposed to remember that it is all a snare and a delusion and no good will come of it. Sooner or later you will have to stop – if you can – and then it will be dreadful. Little Polly Williams from the Ship Inn, Pontypool, danced with the fairies under a crab apple tree on her way home from school for years; she came and went and all was delightful. Polly really seemed to have bucked the trend. But when her visits began to grow less frequent, the fairies – perhaps sensing that soon she would not return at all – treated her with a coldness, and turned their faces from her. Then she knew that something had passed on by, a glory was gone from the days. Polly was one of the lucky ones, she got off very lightly, though the yearning never left her and she always had a limp.

And yet … does it really have to be that way? Is there always a price to pay?

There were two men going past a meadow at Pontcwm. In this meadow there was a huge oak tree, and around the tree there was a bare circle of ground. Not bare because it lay in shade, but because it had been danced bare by the feet of the fairy people, which though light are very persistent. It was springtime, and the two men were walking back from the day's labour and although they were worn out and weary – well, it was springtime. The sun was shining and though they knew it was early, deceptive sunshine and the land was not truly warmed yet, still as they passed by the oak tree they stopped. They looked at one another, and neither of them said any-thing, they just took off their jackets and laid them on the ground beneath the oak tree. They hesitated for a moment, not sure whether they should stretch out on the grass too, there, in the quiet, in the cheating spring sunshine. But instead, what happens is this:

One man gives a little skip – just lifts his foot into the air and stretches his hand out. The other man sways and gives a little sort of shimmy with his hips and they both start to grin at one another and in a split second it is done, they are dancing. And very soon they are not dancing alone, they are moving and swaying amidst a throng of beings, little people! They can only see them from the corner of their eye, but they don't need to see because they can feel. They can move as one – skip, sway, step and turn and turn around beneath the gently rocking branches of the great oak tree. And they dance on and on there, the circle worn bare beneath them. And one of them closes his eyes just for a second, to ground himself in the wonder of it and when he opens them —

Well, when he opened his eyes there was nothing much. Nothing and no one. He was alone beneath the oak tree. There on the ground lay his jacket, where he had dropped it, stained with dirt and dust now, and beside it lay his friend's jacket. He called and called but answer came there none. He waited there by the tree till it was almost dark. Then he picked up both jackets and walked home, clinging to a faint hope that he would find his friend back safe and sound at home, and everything would be as it was before.

But in the village there was no sign of his friend. No one had see him since he left for work that morning. What had become of him? People were quite anxious. They were particularly curious about the jacket. And so after a while the man said, a little shame-faced but frankly enough, that they had both danced beneath the oak tree, in the place worn bare by fairy feet, and they had seen the fairy folk and danced with them, but he had come home alone. Not surprisingly, everyone questioned him at length about all this. They wanted all the details they could get.

'White,' he said. 'They were white, I think ... their clothes and their faces and their hair ... yes, and their eyes were white too ... and they were no higher than my shoulder.'

But the man could say little more, he couldn't find the words for it, he hardly felt sure himself now. He looked at the dusty jacket he carried round with him all the time now and everyone else looked at the jacket too, and they wondered.

'We didn't have a fight – nothing at all like that!' the man said. 'I never killed him, if that's what you're thinking! He just disappeared, that's all. Disappeared. Clean and clever.'

Next day he went back, desperate to find his friend again. He took the jacket, in case his friend was cold. He needed him to come back now, come back and show everyone that he was alright; that he was none the worse for wear, no harm done, no need for suspicion. He stood beneath the branches of the oak tree and waited. Fortunately, he didn't have long to wait. There stood his friend, stepping into focus amidst a throng of glimmering, lilting bodies. He reached out and grabbed his friend's arm, clung to it, put the jacket in his fist, closed his fingers over it.

'They think I'm a murderer,' he said. 'Come back now. Come on, man.'

When the man who had been away with the fairies saw the fear in his friend's eyes he hesitated for a moment, then he stepped forward reluctantly. He nodded. The sea of shimmering bodies ebbed back, sighed a little.

'I'll come and just show my face. Say I'm alright,' he said. 'That's all, mind.'

He put his jacket on and the two men walked home together.

Back in the village the man who had been with the fairies answered all the questions as well as he could.

'White, you could call it. Just up to my shoulder, white clothes, and hair – and eyes.'

Everyone could see perfectly well that he was the same as ever, uninjured and in good spirits, wherever he'd been.

'Lucky escape, probably,' they said. 'Learned your lesson.'

Next morning the two men set off for work. At the meadow called Pontcwm they stopped. By the great oak tree, one stayed on the path and one stepped forward to the circle of ground danced bare by fairy feet. The two men looked at one another and smiled. Shimmering shapes surrounded the man stood beneath the branches. He gave a little skip, and the lilting company disappeared, and him in the midst of them.

He was never seen or heard of again. No bundle of clothes, not even a jacket, no note, no deadly bargains. Just a sideways step, a lilt, a kick of the heel and – gone. They say he must have come to a bad end, some dark destiny, but perhaps he didn't. Perhaps sometimes it is just perfect. Perhaps sometimes it is clean and clever.

22

BAILEY AND THE BANKSMAN

Ironmaster Crawshay 'Cosher' Bailey ruled his realm with – well, an iron fist. Especially when it came to opposing higher rates of pay for his workforce. In common with many powerful entrepreneurs of his era, he did conspicuous 'good works' too. Most of the stories told about him have a slightly rueful tone; the joke is on him, and small victories are sweet.

It is said that Crawshay Bailey was a man who liked to keep a close eye on how everything was progressing at his works. He would spend hours probing and peering into nooks and crannies on the surface and also sometimes he would go down into the mines for a good look round underground. One day he was inspecting Winches Pit when he came across Lewis the Banksman, a worker from Twyncynghordy whose job was to control the descents and ascents of the cage by means of a hand-brake system. Lewis was in the middle of a heated argument with one of the tippers and Bailey immediately waded in and told them to stop arguing and get on with the work they were paid to do, ending by saying, 'Just remember that I am the gaffer here.'

He then declared his intention of going down to inspect the working below ground, and he took his place on the pit cage. The wheels slowly began to revolve and the cage began its descent into the darkness. Then, halfway down, the cage suddenly stopped. There was Crawshay Bailey neither up nor down, neither here nor there, suspended in utter blackness. After he had hung there for a while, peering doubtfully upwards, unable to see anything above or below, a voice came echoing hoarsely down the shaft.

'O Mr Bailey, who is the gaffer now?'

A moment or so later Crawshay Bailey's voice drifted up from the cage.

'O Mr Lewis, you are. You are the gaffer now.'

Only then did Lewis release the brake and continue lowering the cage and Crawshay Bailey to the bottom.

23

RED CLOAK,
BLACK HAT

It was late autumn and the woman was seven months pregnant with her first child. She and her husband were employed in the brass-making trade in Caerleon town, and although they lived and worked alongside one another they had hardly exchanged a single word for days. And by now the woman was feeling that she would be quite happy never to speak to him again.

The silence between them had been growing steadily as the baby grew. Her husband longed for the child, she was fairly sure of that. But there was something that made him edge away quietly from the great curve of her belly. And if she took hold of his hand and held it close to feel the strength of the little feet that were kicking there somewhere in the watery darkness it would only be a moment before he pulled his hand away shyly, softly, remembering some important work that needed doing urgently at the far side of the workshop.

She had grown quieter too, and a little lonelier, sinking deeper within herself. But on this particular evening there were a thousand things she wanted to speak about, a thousand thoughts chasing one another around and around her head. So, with her mind running riot and her husband permanently busying himself with tasks that made conversation impossible, the woman did what was customary under such circumstances and hurried off to spend a few hours with an old friend who lived 'Ultra Pontem' – in the village on the other side of the river.

Her friend, whom she had known all her life, already had two children of her own and once they were safely packed off to bed the two women sat by the fire and ate a whole seedcake between them and debated the at times strange and exasperating ways of men. After a couple of hours in her friend's company the woman felt almost as if the things that had been troubling her didn't really matter after all. Almost. And it was all so pleasant and comforting that she stayed there later than she had meant to but at last, reluctantly, she got to her feet and steeled herself to set off home across the river into town. She tied on her black hat extra firmly, because she could hear how the wind was blowing in the chimney. She lit her lantern from the fire and pulled her red cloak around her, then she hugged her friend as close as she could for as long as she could, then she set off determinedly into the night. It took every ounce of that determination not to turn around and scuttle back in to the friendly fireside.

She had set out from home earlier that day in a drizzle, but now she was returning in a proper storm. Buffeted and blown and shielding her lantern as best she could, she made her way stoutly towards the bridge, which in those days was made of wood, stretching out levelly over the water on ten sturdy piers. The bridge had been built to withstand the flood tides that sometimes came surging along the Usk. While the woman had been sat cosily by the fire with her friend, sharing the concerns of her heart, just such a flood tide had indeed begun to surge, fed by full streams further up in the Breconshire mountains and whipped wilder by the growing storm.

Stepping out onto the bridge with her lantern, she could see nothing of the wild cauldron of water below. She only knew that the sooner she got safely across, the sooner she would be home and warm in bed. She was midway across the bridge when there was a loud creak then an almighty crack and suddenly the world fell away beneath her. The woman dropped straight down into the raging water and the flood swept her away. After the first few seconds of shock, she realised that she must have fallen along with a whole section of the bridge, because she was still holding on to a wooden rail. She was upright, and speeding down the river, riding the waves as if on a crazy raft. The hand that was not holding onto the rail was still clutching the lantern, which amazingly was still alight, though it was flickering wildly. Shielding the lantern as best she could with her body, she balanced, steadying herself as the water rushed and tumbled and thudded all around.

For several moments she travelled on through the darkness in that way, with her one tiny light, still managing to stay upright, still clinging on to the rail. In the midst of the lurching and pounding she thought she felt the child in her belly give a great kick. River water began to pool around her ankles. The idea flashed into her head that maybe she could take off her hat and use it to bail – but that would mean letting go of the rail. Moments later, as she swept past St Julian's, the lantern blew out. Then, for the first time, the woman screamed. With her voice unlocked, she shouted out again and again for help. The storm and the river were so loud that she was afraid her voice would be lost among the din – still, she could see lights being lit, and shutters being opened and people peering out from their bedroom windows as if they had heard her cries. But she was being carried by too fast; she was out of view in an instant. She fell silent again. She told herself that all she had to do was hold on, keep her balance and soon the boatmen of Newport, who were always on watch, would see her and she would be rescued.

As the piece of Caerleon bridge that was now her liferaft approached the bridge at Newport the current rammed it hard into one of the piers, and the woman was shrugged off into the water. Her red cloak billowed out around her and for a moment she floated there, eddying by the bridge pier – just long enough to grab hold of a single beam of wood as it lurched forward out of the debris. Then on she went again, rushing forwards, her black hat bobbing above the wave, her face by turns under and above the water, her arm clamped firmly around the beam.

What lay ahead, she knew, was the swollen mouth of the river and the muddy sea, criss-crossed by currents, where there would be no one to see or hear her.

But still she held tight to the beam as she was carried on through the twisting, turning dark; and she thought of her child within her, and how they both floated now in the darkness with nothing to do but trust.

Then, as the river began to widen into the saltwater channel, a light flashed, somewhere away to the right, and tilting her head back to keep the river out she opened her mouth and called out as loud as she could. The light flashed again, then several small lights clustered together and she could just make out a group of faces peering doubtfully over, not sure of what they were seeing. The woman shouted out again – and suddenly the lights were coming closer. A boat – two boats – were being steered swiftly, skilfully into her path, cutting her off. She was afraid she would have been carried past them but here where the river widened it flowed slower, and soon they were alongside. Hands were grabbing the beam, lashing it fore and aft, rough voices telling her to keep her head, to keep quiet, to hold on. Then she was stretching out her hands, she was being pulled into a small boat, and her knees went from under her then and she sat in a tumble amongst ropes and bailing cups, and only then did she realise that her fingers were still clasped tight around the little waterlogged lantern.

She knew they were smugglers. With much low-voiced cursing, they hurried to unleash the beam again and she watched it rush away, heading for the sea. Then she was taken to shore and hurried up the muddy bank to a small, low shed where she was left on her own, the men melting quickly away into the darkness. In the little shed, a few coals burned in a brazier. She tried to undo the ribbon of her hat but it was in a tight, sodden knot and her fingers trembled and had no strength so instead she peeled off her red cloak and her flannel gown and her drawers, all full of river water. When one of the men returned with a blanket he stood in the doorway for a moment and looked astonished at the woman sat there in the small glow from the fire, naked except for the black hat at a slightly skewed angle, her belly rising in a great swelling curve. He looked at her and he smiled – until, teeth chattering, she had to hold out her hand for the blanket and he remembered himself, and came over and wrapped the blanket around her shoulders. Then he rested his hand lightly on her belly. The woman's eyes met his, but no words passed between them.

24

THE SABBATH
OF THE CHAIR

The Reverend Morgan Howell was preaching at Y Tŷ Round, a little building on the main road from Blackwood to Argoed, when there was a sudden unfortunate occurrence.

Y Tŷ Round was used by the Methodists in the days before the
chapel was built and had no pulpit of any kind, so all preachers
great and small had to stand on a chair to address the congregation, and this is exactly what the Reverend Morgan Howell was
doing. His sermon was building steadily and powerfully, infused
with the passion of conviction that coursed through his being and
the urge to convey it to others, when all at once he overbalanced
and fell off the chair. He did not end up actually sprawled on the
floor, or sustain any physical injury – but he did feel very shaken.
The flow and vigour, the *hwyl* of his sermon, was abruptly cut off
and, despite his best efforts, he could not quite recover it. In the
church meeting that followed, there was a sorrowful discussion
about the accident, and the members of the congregation were
very sympathetic. But Morgan Howell, having had a little time to
consider the matter, said that as far as he was concerned there was
nothing accidental about it. His toppling from the chair in such a
way, he explained in the *seiat*, was the deliberate work of the devil
and he intended to respond to it. He had already had an idea about
what form the response should take.

'As sure had Satan has done this,' said Morgan Howell, 'if I am
spared I will pay him back in his own coin.'

His idea was a neat one. It turned out that in his youth the reverend had been an apprentice in the workshop of a church elder
in Newport, where he had learned the art of cabinet-making. His
response to the devil's challenge would therefore be to make a
pulpit chair. And not just any pulpit chair, but a superior item of
furniture that would serve as a pulpit (with lectern), a communion
table (with flap), a cupboard (with a lock) for the vessels of the
sacrament, and a comfortable seat to rest on, all in one. Above all,
it would be strong and sturdy, both designed and made by Morgan
Howell himself, and it would at a stroke counteract the wiles of
the devil, the possibility of wobbling or toppling, and the strain on
arthritic knees. If it occurred to any members of the congregation
or lay preachers at Y Tŷ Round, pulpit-less for fifteen years, that
Morgan Howell might have made use of his skills a little sooner, no
one mentioned it.

The arrival of the Reverend Morgan Howell's chair was keenly awaited. And as all things come to those who wait, so at last the chair arrived. It was generally declared to be as splendid and thoroughly fit-for-purpose as Morgan Howell had envisaged. It seemed almost to the elders that this chair was of divine pattern, the inspiration and instructions for its making given to Morgan Howell much as the pattern of the Tabernacle had been given to Moses. That may have been partly the reason why, after some discussion, it was decided not to start using the chair straight away but to keep it until the next occasion when Morgan Howell himself was to preach there. Until then, the congregation would be addressed from an ordinary chair as usual.

And so a covering was carefully placed over the pulpit chair and it was put safely away in a side room. Then an announcement was made that there would be a special consecration day, the Sabbath of the Chair, on the occasion of Morgan Howell's next visit, when the chair would be formally dedicated to sacred service.

The Sabbath arrived and so did Morgan Howell; 'And,' as some of the church fathers said afterwards, 'God Himself came with him.' On his arrival, everyone noted that Morgan Howell looked pale and worn – so sickly that his appearance drew tears from the eyes of his old friends in the congregation. Some felt worried that he might collapse before he could even begin to deliver his sermon. But without speaking to anyone, or listening to cautious counsel, Morgan Howell made his way 'as one seeing the Invisible', straight to the newly installed pulpit chair and stepped up to his place at the lectern. He covered his face for a moment or two in silent prayer and then began a heartfelt hymn.

As Morgan Howell proceeded through the introductory part of the service, took his text and entered into his sermon, his apparent bodily weakness seemed to fall from him. He began to glow with a passion that flowed from him in eloquent streams, overwhelming and filling the hearts and minds of all who heard, in a way that the church elders said afterwards, 'made them to forget themselves'.

Morgan Howell stood squarely at the pulpit chair he himself had fashioned in response to the devil's challenge and felt that he was forever safe and sound.

'It is immaterial to me,' he said, 'if the Judgement come before tomorrow morning and Newport should be in flames. I shall be able to dance on its ashes. Because the Rock of Ages is under my feet!'

The listening congregation did not waste time considering any possible ramifications of Newport in flames because in that moment they also felt sure of the solid ground beneath their feet; and on that ground they danced and shook with passion, old Kitty Williams dancing like a young girl and shouting out for joy 'Sing, sing, my soul, sing out from your solid foundation!' and '*Gogoniant!* Glory!' called Morgan Howell throughout.

> *Am Graig yr iachawdwriaeth*
> *Fy enaid egwan cân;*
> *Y sylfaen fawr safadwy*
> *A'r hyfryd Gongl-faen …*

Later, when the elders of the church came to describe the scene that day, one by one they found themselves falling silent, as if their tongues were cleaving to the roof of their mouth. And when they did speak it was in low tones, and few words. 'Very terrible,' they said, 'and we cannot forget it'. As if it was almost too much to bear – too solid, too tremendous. And a holy hush fell over the Sabbath of the Chair, vivid though it burned in the hearts and minds of all who were there.

The pulpit chair stayed a long time in Y Tŷ Round and in the chapel that took its place. Sturdy, plain and solid, keeping its sacrament safe and sound.

25

RHAMANTA! (OR NANSI LLWYD AND THE DOG OF DARKNESS)

Deep below the ground, in the mountains around the parish of Aberystruth, the old stone mothers sit together and consider the ways of those above ground. Brief human lives and intrigues catch their attention now and then, and wise and ancient though they are, they will still listen with some interest to young women talking about how exciting life is.

One day a couple of hundred years ago Nansi Llwyd and her friends Gwenno and Siân were discussing that very subject. All three of them were farm-daughters and their farms were just beyond shouting distance of one another, Gwenno and Siân on one slope of the mountain, Nansi on the other. They had played together as girls, skipped and searched for frogspawn in spring, and frightened themselves silly on winter nights listening to tales of the Gwyllgi, the ferocious black dog from the Otherworld who roams the hills. And when the days of skipping and frogspawn came to an end their friendship continued and they took every chance they got after the long hours of farm work to meet and dream and chatter and dance and quarrel. Their usual meeting place was by an old hawthorn tree that grew in a sheltered spot on the mountainside, at a convenient point midway between their farms. By the time they were sixteen, their meetings – as well as almost all of the time they spent apart – were taken up with something wonderful. That something was *Rhamanta*. The exciting, death-defyingly audacious, sweet and tender matter of finding your very own love story to slip into forever. All three of them knew from their long walks and talks on the hillside that they were ready. Gwenno, who was two months older than the other two and a natural leader, said one day as they sat under the hawthorn tree, 'I am every inch ready for love!'

Then Siân said that as far as she was concerned a husband could come along as soon as he liked and the sooner the better, and Nansi said yes, she too was more than ready for *something to happen*.

They'd already decided to scorn the whole business of love potions, on the grounds that it was beneath their dignity and unnecessary. But they felt it might be useful to get some clues as to what – or who – destiny had in store for them. So they began to listen at doors and seek advice from some of the older women who could be approached about these things, or the occasional traveller who might pass by, from the distant wilds of Herefordshire or Haverfordwest. Siân's cousin's great-aunt from Gilwern favoured placing a large iron key in a Bible opened at the Book of Ruth, then lifting the Bible by placing a forefinger under the key whilst reciting a certain verse. If the key stayed steady the signs were good, if it twisted they were interesting, if the Bible dropped, well that was that.

But Nansi, Siân and Gwenno all felt that this method was a bit outdated. So they used their common sense, ignored any bits of advice that didn't suit them, and came up with a plan for carrying out three interesting and reliable divination tests. The *Rhamanta* would begin with several months of night-time preparation. Starting at Calan Gaeaf on the threshold of winter, Gwenno began to sleep with a large bunch of maidenhair fern in her pillow. Siân placed smaller bunches of seven herbs under her bedsheet (this was her family's own secret, so she would not be persuaded to say exactly which herbs she used). And as for Nansi, from the beginning of November she slept on a mattress stuffed with the finest oat straw and rowan leaves, saved especially for the purpose. And so throughout the winter months the three girls who had made their beds continued to lie in them, inviting dreams; and all the time the mountain mothers lay deep in watchful darkness below them just as they had below the girls' mothers, and their mothers' mothers before them.

When spring came budding into view, it was time for the first test. Just before dawn one morning in March the girls met by the hawthorn tree, and there they each put a small piece of slate on the ground, placed a snail in the middle of the slate and put an earthenware bowl upside down over the top. Then they left all three snails in solitary confinement and headed home to begin the day's work. At dusk, they met again by the tree as arranged. It was drizzling but the three of them stood hugging themselves with excitement, looking down at the three little pots in keen anticipation. The sense of fate that hung in the air was so strong that it was a whole minute before any of them could pluck up the courage to look. Then Gwenno, feeling the responsibility of seniority, reached out her hand and –

'I knew it!'

A fine, shining snail trail twisted across the slate and it was prac-
tically undeniable that it formed the letters S and P. The loop in the
P was clear as anything. It could only be the sign that Siôn Prys,
Siôn of the golden hair and the heart-melting smile, was Gwenno's
destined husband (a fact she had long suspected).

Encouraged by Gwenno's luck, Siân quickly turned her pot over.
Here the fine silver trail was a bit harder to decipher. The three of
them squatted down and peered and puzzled for some time. An M
perhaps? Or a W? An N? Several names of local lads came to mind
– but which one was actually indicated here? Siân said she 'had her
suspicions' but in the end they had to admit that really Siân's test
was promising but inconclusive.

Hoping for greater clarity, Nansi then turned over her pot.
When she did so, silence fell, and the three young women stood
in the fading light looking at the snail, who sat stock still on an
unmarked piece of slate. Nansi checked the upturned pot but that
also bore no trace of an initial. Not so much as a sliver of silver!
Not a quarter inch of snail trail! Gwenno squeezed Nansi's arm.

'Oooh, yours is still wrapped in mystery!' she said.

'Or you just got a lazy snail,' said the ever-pragmatic Siân.

Still, all three of them agreed that this was only ever intended to
be a preliminary test. There was plenty of time for further inves-
tigations in the six weeks still to go before the beginning of May
– *Calan Mai*, when lovers' hopes blossom or are blighted. Gwenno
and Siân were soon hurrying back down the hill for home, but
Nansi lingered a bit longer, looking at the stubbornly blank bit of
slate and the stationary snail, which she picked up and sent into
orbit over the hawthorn tree, to teach it a lesson. Then she walked
home with a tight feeling growing in her chest. *Rhamanta* …

Three weeks later the three young women met at noon, this
time up in the little hayloft at Siân's. They had collected apple tree
twigs and lengths of wool and these they knotted to make a ladder,
using the twigs as rungs. They were at work for a while before
the ladder was long enough, and they talked in excited whispers
as they worked, because this test would show how the land lay in
the business of romancing for a whole year. Once the ladder had

reached the required length, they rolled it carefully into a ball. Gwenno was designated first try, and she leaned out and unwound the ball, lowering the ladder carefully down. Once it had touched the ground she waited for a moment, took a deep breath, fixed her eyes on the horizon and began winding the ladder back up, saying these words in a steady lilting tone:

Fi sy'n dirwyn, pwy sy'n dala ... fi sy'n dirwyn, pwy sy'n dala? ('I am winding, who is holding ... I am winding, who is holding?')

Before the ladder was halfway back up, there in the distance but clear as daylight, golden-haired Siôn Prys passed by along the track, and though they couldn't quite see his smile at that distance they knew it was bound to be more heart-melting than ever. Gwenno, who had just about had the presence of mind not to drop the ladder, glowed with delight. The thing that she had long known in her heart was now certain beyond any doubt. *Rhamanta!* Gwenno and Siôn, a golden couple already bound together in the best love story.

Siân then began to lower the ladder.

Fi sy'n dirwyn, pwy sy'n dala ... fi sy'n dirwyn, pwy sy'n dala?

As she wound she scanned the hillside, but there was no sight of anyone. Just as the ladder was nearing the top a voice came drifting over the hill, laughing and calling out to another. Someone was passing by – they all heard him, but he was out of sight round the side of the hill, his voice carried only for a moment by the wind. Still, it was a sign. Tantalising! The girls couldn't discuss this exciting turn of events because the ladder test had to be carried out in silence apart from the necessary verse, so Siân had no choice but to finish winding the ball and pass it on to Nansi. She unwound it to its full length.

Fi sy'n dirwyn, pwy sy'n dala ... fi sy'n dirwyn, pwy sy'n dala?

All three of them scanned the hillside, straining to listen. Nansi herself hardly dared to breath. There was nothing. There wasn't even a breeze. Nothing moved on the hill. No one was holding. And the ladder was fully wound in, between Nansi's hands. Gwenno and Siân, each wrapped into their own story, hugged their friend magnanimously. 'Remember, it's just for a year,' they said. And anyway, they still had time to try the water-in-basin test, which everyone agreed was the strongest test of all.

Two weeks later, Gwenno was host to Nansi, Siân and three earthenware basins, one filled with clear spring water, one with cloudy water from the pond and one filled with nothing at all. The atmosphere was solemn and tense. The water-in-basin test was a weighty matter and they knew it, because whereas the ladder test gave indications for the year ahead, the water-in-basin test stood for a lifetime. Gwenno, whose confidence was by now unshakeable, stood pale and proud as the scarf was tied around her eyes. Her hand went like an arrow to its target and her fingers dabbled in the bowl of clear spring water. She would marry a bachelor. Of course; there had been no doubt. The basins were swivelled around while Siân's blindfold was secured in place. Siân made a nervous grab. Her fingers found the pond-water. She sighed and laughed out loud. So, there was to be no bachelor for her, but there was *someone*. Perhaps a widower? Or maybe her story would be something more complicated? But whatever lay in store, Siân was beginning to feel more than ready for it.

And then it was Nansi's turn. And if you think you're pretty sure how this is going to go – so was Nansi. Gwenno and Siân tied on her blindfold, swivelled the position of the three bowls again. Nansi stretched out a hand and her fingers grasped – nothing. The empty basin. A bitter taste came into her mouth and a tear stung her eye beneath the blindfold. There was nothing more to be said, then. Brushing aside Gwenno and Siân's sympathies, Nansi hurried off and ran every step of the way home, her heart pounding in her chest. She had known, she had always known! She flung herself on her oat straw and rowan leaf bed and fell at once into an exhausted, dreamless sleep. And all around, the whole circle of mountain mothers watched, nodded, sighed and spread their stony hands wide. *Rhamanta ...*

Next morning, Nansi woke feeling strangely defiant – and with a plan. Maybe a loveless fate awaited her, but there was still a week to go until May Day. She, Nansi Llwyd, would carry out one more test. She knew exactly what she was going to do – although it wouldn't be easy. First, she would have to find a pullet who hadn't yet begun to lay, and coax it to produce its first egg. That egg would then have to be broken in two, one half-shell filled with salt, the other with flour, and a cake be baked with the egg, salt and flour. One half of the cake would have to be eaten before bed, the other half placed under her pillow. Then at some point during the night, the destined lover would appear and offer a by then much-needed drink of water. Gwenno and Siân had rejected this test on the grounds that it was far too fiddly. But that didn't matter because they weren't going to know. Much though she loved them, Nansi didn't think she could tolerate one more ounce of their sympathy. No, she would carry out this test in private and the results would be hers alone to ponder.

The main difficulty was that most of the pullets had been laying for weeks already – but there was one last scrawny one who hadn't, and who had therefore been earmarked for the pot. Nansi spent the next few days lavishing her time and affection on this bird. She saved crumbs from the table, dug worms from the potato patch, sat the pullet in her lap, crooned songs of encouragement to it and stroked it until at last it could resist no longer. On the morning before May Day it laid an egg then and there as it sat in Nansi's lap. Hope sprung up in Nansi's heart. This was surely a good omen – a thing that Nansi sorely needed by now. She stood by the kitchen table and broke the pullet's egg deftly in two. She baked the cake with the salt and flour, tied half into the left foot of her stocking and put it under her pillow. She ate the remaining half cake and climbed into her oat straw bed. The salty taste had already made her thirsty, and it was a long time before she got to sleep. *Rhamanta ... Rhamanta ...*

At last she sank into a dark and troubled dream, where she went down to the stream for water and found that it had dried into a crawling slime. So she went to the well and wound down the bucket, but it came up empty and the rope slipped and burned her hands.

Nansi woke with her heart bleak and heavy and her throat parched. Since no one had come in her dream to bring her water she poured and drank three glasses for herself from the pitcher on the dressing stand. So that was it then. She, Nansi Llwyd, had a name that no lover would ever whisper. A heart that would never beat alongside another! Nansi pulled the oat straw mattress from her bed and watched it spill out over the floor. A cold fury began to grow inside her. She spread open her shawl and gathered the oat straw into it, throwing in the squashed half-shell of cake from under her pillow. Then she tied the shawl up as small and tight as she could, tucked it under her arm and set off. She would throw the whole lot from the top of the mountain ridge and let the wind take it and that would be an end to *Rhamanta* for Nansi Llwyd.

Now, Nansi had walked up that mountain path countless times, since she had first learned to toddle. She'd gone surefooted day and night and in all weathers; she could have done it blindfold without a stumble. So she could never really say why it was that halfway up the path she suddenly tripped and went tumbling, rolling over and over back down the hill a hundred yards or more, still clutching her bundle. She only stopped when her leg struck sharply against a large rock that stood as a waymarker beside the broader track that lead around the foot of the hill. As soon as the world had stopped spinning, and the land and the sky were in more or less their right places again, Nansi got to her feet. Her left leg where it had struck the rock would have a lovely bruise from hip to knee, but nothing was broken.

With grim determination she was just turning to make her way back up the hill again when she felt a sudden trembling and thudding beneath her feet. A split second later she heard the pounding of a horse's hooves, and a whinnying squeal of terror. Bearing down on her at breakneck gallop along the track came a riderless grey horse. Nansi had just enough time to step back as the horse thundered past her, its eyes wide and rolling, the reins slapping loose against its neck. Nansi saw that it was a beautiful, fine dappled mare. The finest she had ever seen, and the most frightened.

Nansi watched as the mare thundered on down the path that rounded the hill then, instinctively, she turned to look again in the direction from which it had come. For a moment there was nothing – an almost uncanny silence.

Nansi wondered if should she follow the mare and try to catch it, calm it? Or should she set off the other way and see what had frightened it so badly, or if there was a rider lying injured or worse? Or should she just get on up the hill and cast her miserable bundle to the wind once and for all?

As she stood hesitating, along the track in the direction from which the dappled mare had appeared, a dark mist came blowing. There was a deep, roaring growl and bounding towards her out of the mist came a huge black hound. Its jowls were streaked with saliva, its eyes burned red-hot coals – a black dog, yes, but more than that, a dog the sight of which turned the noon sunshine dim. Shadows streamed from it into the air, blackening the world. And Nansi knew that she had come face to face with the *Gwyllgi* – the hound whose path it was fatal to cross, the hound from the world below – the Dog of Darkness.

Nansi stood still as the *Gwyllgi* hurtled forwards and she knew that in a moment she would be engulfed. She felt the dim, choking clouds of nothingness that flowed and eddied around, as if the creature was draining light into itself. Her hands were still clutching the tightly wrapped shawl full of oat straw and rowan leaves, that were really just wisps of nothing.

'Well!' said Nansi. 'If I am to be nothing and no one, with a name that no lover ever calls, then so be it. You may take me as you find me.'

And as the Dog of Darkness took a gigantic leap towards her, Nansi stepped forward into its path and flung out her shawl. The shawl floated for a moment, its contents spilling into the dark shadows that streamed in all directions from the leaping dog. Nansi closed her eyes and waited for the terrible jaw-snap that would drag her down into the Underworld. There was a slipping, skidding sound …

Nansi opened her eyes. Sitting on his haunches in a scattered circle of oat straw, rowan leaves, salty cake crumbs and bits of eggshell, panting and looking expectantly towards her was the *Gwyllgi*. Its coat glossy black but no longer streaming with shadow, its eyes bright but not burning fire. And there they both were, for a moment or so. Nansi Llwyd and the Dog of Darkness, on the old hillside, beside the track, regarding one another.

The Dog got to its feet and made to step out of the circle towards Nansi. Nansi raised her hand and at once the Dog sat down again, and waited. Then Nansi heard a whinnying sound, clear and loud but not terrified like before. She called out, clear and steady, '*Hee … ei, dere di 'nghaseg i, heee-ei …*' and slowly the grey mare came trotting back up the track. And though the mare saw the Dog, if she felt fear she felt Nansi's call more strongly, and came to her hand.

Nansi took hold of the reins lightly and lead the beautiful grey mare on along the track. She called to the Dog, who jumped out of the circle of straw and leaves and trotted along at her heels. Very soon they came upon the fallen rider, who was sat on the ground, rubbing his head. Nansi knew at once that she had not seen this young man before. She would have remembered. As they approached, he looked up and stared at the horse, the Dog and the young woman walking between them. He hadn't seen her before. He would have remembered.

He asked, 'Who are you?'

And she replied, 'I am Nansi Llwyd. This walking by my side is the Dog of Darkness. And this is your mare, I suppose.'

The man got to his feet and said his name, and his mare's name, then he took hold of the reins and the little group began to walk back together along the path. When they reached the place where the circle of straw had lain there was nothing to be seen because the mountain breeze had already carried it away.

'Where are you headed?' asked Nansi.

'I have a message to take to a cousin of mine who lives not far from here,' the young man answered. 'And when that is done, I intend to go and see what the world may have to offer one such as myself.'

'I am on my way to the top of the mountain,' said Nansi. 'I expect I will see you as you ride on your way, and I'll see if any other hounds of darkness come to trouble you.'

And they both turned to look at the Dog of Darkness. But it had disappeared into the place of mists, the Otherworld that is its home.

'If I return on this same path,' said the young man, 'will I find you?'

'There's an old hawthorn tree halfway up the far slope of the hill,' said Nansi. 'You might meet me there.'

The young man nodded, mounted his horse and rode on.

Nansi did not linger to watch him go, she turned and went striding up the mountain side, the whinberry leaves and the short mountain grass springy beneath her step. When she reached the top she watched the young man and the dappled mare until they disappeared from view in the lee of the mountain. She did not doubt that his return would be soon.

'And we will see,' said Nansi, 'what the world may have to offer one such as myself.'

Deep below the ground, in the mountains around the parish of Aberystruth, the old stone mothers sit together and consider the ways of those above ground. Brief human lives and intrigues catch their attention, now and then, and wise and ancient though they are, they will still listen with some interest when the young women talk about how exciting life is.

26

THE GIANT

In days long gone by, the wooded and beautiful lands of Gwent were home to a good few giants. It's hard to say much about them now – where they lived, what their concerns were. Probably they weren't very good and they weren't very bad, they were the same sort of mixed bag you might find today amongst your neighbours, or your own family. And I don't know whether they were hand-some or ugly, but their mother loved the bones of them. They were, after all, her flesh and blood. She rocked them and held them close for a very long time in her own deep, earthy way before ever they were allowed to venture out on their own.

Still, all mothers must release their hold in the end, and Mother under the Earth is no exception, and her sons went on their wandering ways at last. They wandered off in different directions and they went quite slowly, taking notice of things around them and savouring their steps. They liked the feel of the forest floor under their feet; the way the leaves tickled and the wet squidgy pools between their toes made them smile. People who move slowly and smile to themselves are sometimes thought of as slow-witted, which might be why Giants are often said to be a bit *twp*. But it is not necessarily the case.

Anyhow, one by one the Giants moved on, out and away, dispersing into the hills and woodlands on their own adventures. Bwch and Clidda and Trogi – and others whose names are long lost. But there is one who, although his name is lost, has a story that would not go away. He was the Giant brother who moved slowest of all, and looked around him the most, and wiggled his toes longest in the soggy drifts of last year's fallen leaves. He wandered for a long time in the wooded lands of Aberbargoed, where the old county borders of Monmouthshire and Glamorganshire meet. There he found a lot to look at, and a lot that made him smile. And he lingered so long and looked at everything so slowly and deeply, that of all the Giant brothers he was the only one ever to see – *actually see* – the Queen of the Fairies.

She was not easily seen. She was tall enough (though not as tall as the Giant), only the light shone right through her so that she didn't seem to take up any space at all. And since something that doesn't take up any space can't really be there, most people who caught a fleeting half-glimpse of the Queen of the Fairies from the corner of their eye, and might perhaps have seen her if they had stood still for long enough, just thought she was a momentary trick of the light. So, the Queen of the Fairies was not used to being seen, and so, of course, she wasn't used to being looked at. And she certainly wasn't used to being stared at, let alone spoken to. So when on a fine spring morning she suddenly became aware

of the steady gaze of the Giant upon her, and he actually said
'Hello, rainbow', it came as quite a shock. She was so surprised she
didn't say anything at all at first. She just stood there as the Giant's
smile slowly broadened until it almost split his face in two. When
at last she managed to speak (her voice was surprisingly low and
resonant for one so translucent) what she said was 'GUARDS!!!'
Within seconds her loyal retinue were at her side; lanky, highly
trained, armed with daggers and ready to use them. Pausing just
long enough to glare menacingly at the Giant, they surrounded the
Fairy Queen and then they all disappeared as one – perhaps into
thin air, it was hard to tell.

And that should really have been the last the Giant and the
Fairy Queen ever saw of one another, but it wasn't. Far from it.
Quite soon afterwards she appeared to the Giant again in exactly
the same spot, where he was still sat with his back against an oak
tree. You would almost think she had returned hoping he would
still be there – if that hadn't been such a preposterous idea. And
even before the Giant had time to notice her, the Queen of the
Fairies said 'Hello, Giant' and she was gratified by the look of utter
delight that crossed the Giant's face.

They met quite often after that, in the same spot, or thereabouts.
They would greet one another politely, and they'd soon be chatting
away happily. And apart from that very first time, when after all
she had been a little wrong-footed, the Queen of the Fairies never
once called for her guards when she was in the Giant's company.

But the guards were keeping a Very Close Eye on the Giant.
In fact, they had him under surveillance at all times, though they
didn't feel the need to bother the Fairy Queen with this information. Funnily enough, keeping an eye on the Giant wasn't as easy
as it sounded, because although you mightn't think it, Giants are
really quite good at camouflage. It's not just the greeny-browny
earthy woodland colours they wear (which is a similar colour to
their skin). It's more the way the shadows fall across their features,
making edges and shapes seem uncertain. And, of course, they
do move very slowly and keep quite still for long periods of time.
That's how the stories arose that seem so unlikely on the face of it,

of people out for a walk and climbing a hill and hearing a strange rumble beneath them then suddenly realising that they've actually been walking up the belly of a Giant, stretched out on the land, as still as anything. Or staring into the double cavern of a Giant's nostrils and being sneezed halfway across the county. It's all down to the camouflage and the stillness.

However, the Fairy Queen's guards were extremely thorough in their methods of surveillance. First of all, they sent out scouts to establish whether he was the only Giant in the immediate vicinity. He was; by that time his brothers were long gone. Then they began compiling lists of his favourite haunts, building up a dossier of his habits, his usual routines, his favourite paths through the woods and so on. They were wise enough to deploy only their best scouts in tracking the Giant, and he never spotted them. Not until it was way too late. The Giant's meetings with the Fairy Queen – date, time, location, duration and nature – were especially carefully noted. The Captain of the Guard made it crystal clear that the safety of the Queen at all times and in all places was their Chief Primary Responsibility and he personally took his duty extremely seriously. No Captain in the history of Faerydom had ever let the Queen come to harm and he certainly didn't intend to be the first.

From their second meeting by the oak tree – and if truth be told, probably from the very first – the Queen of the Fairies and the Giant knew that they loved one another. The Captain of the Guard worked this out for himself pretty soon too, but the problem was that he simply did not know what to do about it. There were no guidelines to follow, nothing in the manual, and no hint that a Captain of the Guard had ever had to deal with such a situation before. He deeply resented being put in this predicament. All he knew, with a savage certainty that burned way down in his belly, was that it was not on for a Fairy Queen and a Giant to become intimate. No. It was not correct, and it was not necessary.

So, for some time round-the-clock surveillance of the Giant was maintained and the Captain's dossier got fuller and fuller of recorded trysts.

Meanwhile, hanging from the boughs of the trees throughout the beautiful woodlands of Aberbargoed, bright flower garlands and lovers' knots began to appear, left by the Fairy Queen for the Giant, and by the Giant for the Fairy Queen. Delicious laughter was heard with increasing frequency – anyone passing by might hear it, the Captain thought to himself angrily – though nobody did. And then, in the early hours of one moonlit morning when a scout reported back that the Giant and the Queen of the Fairies were lying quite close to one another inside a fairy ring beneath the beech trees and neither of them was wearing any clothes, the Captain of the Guards felt that things could not be allowed to continue and action must be taken. The question was, what action? He would have to tread carefully. He knew he couldn't just go barging in making accusations. After all, this was the Fairy Queen; he took his orders from her, not the other way round, appealing though that thought might be. So after a good deal of pondering he came up with what he considered to be a tactful plan. He suggested to the Fairy Queen that she might like to go on a progress, and visit some of the nearby woodlands or valleys. Perhaps even call in on one of the Fairy Kings beyond the hills? After all, she hadn't been on her travels for such a long time and so many people were longing to see her.

But when the Fairy Queen just smiled vaguely and dismissed him with a wave, the Captain knew, as he had suspected all along, that other measures would be called for.

He selected members of the Guard and sent them out as *agents provocateurs* amongst the scattered farmsteads that dotted the land in those days. Disguised as passing travellers, they started conversations with the woodland people about how big and clumsy the Giant's feet were, and how easy it was for him to squash things without even noticing. Not to mention how much the Giant ate! And whilst these conversations were getting under way, they set about fabricating a trail of destruction. They staged covert raids on grain stores, stripped the best produce from vegetable gardens, left a huge 'footprint' or two, putting the Giant firmly in the frame. And it soon became a well-known fact that Giants ate human and fairy babies whenever they could get their hands on them.

And all this time the Giant and the Fairy Queen continued to meet and talk and smile and lie in fairy rings, quite oblivious to the waves of discontent being stirred up around them. But the Guard had done their job all too well. One full moonlit night, they fermented such a discord amongst the woodland folk that a dozen or so of them went marching through the forest to confront the Giant and give him a piece of their mind and present him with a list of grievances. Arriving at the same time as the woodland folk, the Guard entered the clearing where the Giant was stood quietly looking up at the night sky. The Captain gave orders for the delivery not of a list of grievances, but a hail of fairy arrows. Each arrow was tipped with a poison that would fell an ox. Even so, the elite archers of the Guards had to send a dozen hails of arrows into the Giant's body before he stumbled and swayed. He managed to take a last few giant steps towards the oak tree – their special meeting place, where he hoped to get one last look at the beloved Fairy Queen, the lady of his heart, the rainbow of the land.

And that's where she found him, next morning, his hair soaked with dew, a bright garland still in his hand that he had made for her, the deadly fairy darts all melted away.

The Captain of the Guard did eventually persuade the Fairy Queen to go off for a rest cure. They didn't come back for a long time – if they ever did. The woodland people avoided the spot where the Giant lay; years passed, and every autumn leaf-fall buried him deeper, and roots of trees twisted all around him. After a time, folk just forgot about him. But his mother loved the bones of him. He was her flesh and blood. She rocked him and held him close for a very long time in her own deep, earthy way.

Over many years, more and more little farms and cottages began to appear in the woodland. And in time a great stink began to arise from the place where the Giant's body lay long buried and forgotten. It grew so bad that no one wanted to live with it any longer and they took mattocks and shovels and went to investigate what it was that stank so badly. When they found the blackened body of the Giant they set it on fire, reasoning that fire purifies. But this fire blazed and it blazed, so hot and bright and long that they wondered at the sight. And so, hesitatingly at first then in great loads, they began to take little blackened pieces of the Giant's body back to their hearths, where they burned, hotly and truly, steadily and dependably. Stories gathered round with them as they sat by the flickering flames of their fires, and as fireside and story have always gone together, so it continued, old as the love of the Mother in the Earth for her sons, warm as the love of the Giant and his Fairy Queen, the dark body and the bright rainbow of the land.

27

RICH MAN, POOR MAN, BEGGAR MAN, THIEF

All these titles have been bestowed on William Jones in telling the story of how he came to found a free school and almshouses in the town of Monmouth four hundred years ago. The twists and hiccups in the story might have arisen because of the sudden jolt tales sometimes undergo when they cross borders – especially when they zig-zag back and forth several times. William Jones, it is agreed, was born in Newland in the Forest of Dean just four miles from the town of Monmouth, over the border in England. But a rollercoaster of good and bad fortune sent him to and fro, and in the end it was the Monmouth side of the border in particular who found him to be a golden son.

William was not particularly high or low born, and he was just a young lad when he left Newland for Monmouth to widen his horizons – very slightly. And whether he was intended for an apprenticeship or not, story has it that before long he was working right at the bottom of the employment ladder as a boot-boy in The Kings Head pub. He was a polite and friendly lad, quick on the uptake, a fast learner, and he was well-liked by the regulars – those who took any notice of him, that is. Joe King, the itinerant shoemaker who had a regular watering-hole at the pub, took to sitting with Will and casting a professional eye over the pile of boots and shoes that he always had waiting to be cleaned and polished. The two struck up quite a friendship, with Joe pointing out the differences between the quality workman-ship in the boots made to last a lifetime and the shoddier-made, cheaper pairs, and Will in turn musing on how unlikely it was on his current wages that he would be able to afford either kind any time soon. And Will and Joe mused together on the irony of the life of a boot-boy. The most exquisite, worthy, well-made and serviceable items of footwear might pass through his hands every day, but his own feet there on the bottom rung of the employ-ment ladder were often covered by little more than outgrown scraps of leather, with boot blacking disguising white skin that peeped through the holes. Still, both Will and Joe King were of a naturally cheerful disposition and were agreed that when you were at the bottom, the only way was up.

Everything would probably have progressed well enough for Will if he hadn't fallen foul of love-sickness. But he did. It was love at first sight, naturally. In the time-honoured manner, Will was struck by Cupid's arrow, which sent ardour racing through him like a wild fire and there he was, fallen sick as sick could be for the love of a young woman who had no interest in boot-boys, however cheerful or however cute they were. Only it was a long while before Will realised that this was the case. He went through all the stages of dogged devotion; daring to hope, clutching at straws, glimpsing good omens and hidden meanings in the briefest of smiles. Then, finally, despair and the sickening crashing to the ground of dreams built on nothing more substantial than wishful thinking. When the realisation finally came that he was Not Enough it hit William hard. His first idea was to drown himself in the river, but he loved the water and was a strong swimmer, so he progressed very quickly to his second idea, which was to get as far away as possible from anywhere that had been graced by the young woman's beauty and tainted by his own misery. He wouldn't walk into the river – but he could walk off into the night. Unfortunately for Will, although he certainly could walk off into the night, he would have trouble keeping on walking for any distance, because his shoes were in pieces, and it was well into October so most roads were already becoming miracles of mud.

Now, Joe King had noticed Will growing white-faced and stricken-looking, but he hadn't known what to say, so their conversation had stuck to boots and shoes, as usual. But as days passed, conversation between the two of them began to fizzle out earlier and earlier in the evenings. Then one evening, Will didn't appear at all and Joe stumped off to his bed early, in the corner where the landlord always put him up a mattress behind a little curtain. As usual, Joe had left out a couple of pairs of boots he was working on. Amongst them was one pair that Will had especially admired; a sturdy pair, expertly made and now expertly repaired by Joe and ready to be returned to their owner. When Joe got up next morning to start work, he noticed straight away that this particular pair of boots was missing. Also missing, if the shouts and curses of the landlord were anything to go by, was boot-boy William Jones. And if there had been any doubt as to the connection between the missing boy and the missing boots, that doubt was settled by a little note that Joe King found tucked into his toolbox. It said, *'I will pay for them do not doubt it W.J.'*

Joe felt the shock, and he pondered. The landlord and the customers who had thought well enough of Will were taken aback,
said they wouldn't have thought it of him and were soon calling
him all the names under the sun. Still, boot-boys weren't hard
to come by, and by the end of the week a new young lad from
Mitchel Troy was whistling his way through the muddy piles of
footwear and Will's sudden disappearance was already old news.
Although for Joe King, who had to make good the loss of a valu-
able pair of boots to a trusted customer, the matter took a little
longer to put to rest. In the end, Joe achieved peace of mind by
deciding to view the money he had had to pay out as a temporary
inconvenience. More importantly, he decided to consider the loss
of his friend Will in the same way. And though everyone else
thought Joe would never see money, boots or boot-boy again, Joe
had made up his mind that the debt would be repaid sooner or
later, because Will had said it would. As a result, Joe slept easily
in his bed at night – though he missed his long philosophical
discussions with Will in the back bar, amongst the boot blacking
and the scrapers.

And the years came and went. And there was no money for Joe,
and no boots and no William Jones.

Thirty years later, a poor man in a ragged coat, his feet bound
in rags, his back bent double, came trembling into the village of
Newland and made his way haltingly to the well in the yard of
the little house where the Jones family had lived in years gone by.
The woman of the house set the dog on the bedraggled stranger,
who limped off without a word and collapsed onto the bench
outside the Ostrich Inn in the centre of the village. He sat there for
the rest of the day, speaking to no one and no one speaking to him.
As dusk came on and it was abundantly clear that this was one customer who was not about to order a drink, he was hoisted to his feet
and given a shove in the direction of the poorhouse. Still no drink of
water had passed his lips. At the poorhouse he was required to give
his name and parish. He gave his name as Will Jones and his parish
of birth as Newland. But on discovering how long he had been away

the poorhouse was reluctant to accept him as its responsibility and would not take him in. Instead it sent him on to Monmouth, being the place he had left so many years before. And the poorhouse at Monmouth did take him in, and gave him some water to drink, some bread to eat and a pauper's suit to wear. After a day or so, the man went in search of Joe King and found him at work at The King's Head. The two men, both bent over like bows, talked for a while and Joe, when asked if he remembered a young lad called William Jones, smiled briefly, and said he remembered him well enough. When asked whether he still believed that the debt owed for the boots would be repaid Joe simply said yes, and bent to his work again. He wouldn't sin his soul, he said, by begrudging a poor despairing lad a decent pair of boots to walk away in. Next day, the newest pauper absconded from Monmouth poorhouse still wearing the suit of clothes he had been issued with on arrival.

It was a month later when a coach drew up outside the poorhouse and a tall, broad-shouldered man got out. He walked to the door of the house, his back straight as a poplar tree, a newly laundered pauper's suit done up in a parcel. When it had been delivered, he walked to The King's Head and as he had hoped, found Joe King there. Now, though one man stood straight the other's back was still bent. But Joe looked keenly up at Will as he spoke. Within moments he believed indeed that not only was the trembling pauper and the upright man who stood before him one and the same person – but that person was William Jones. The purse of gold William held out to Joe paid the debt several times over, if seeing him again were not repayment enough.

The people of Newland do not consider that they are particularly intolerant or unkind. The people of Monmouth would probably admit that they do not have a monopoly on generosity and trust. But though he left money to assist the poor of both places, it was in Monmouth that the now wealthy and altruistic haberdasher William Jones founded a free grammar school. Perhaps he just preferred the town. And some stories do undergo sudden jolts when they cross borders.

PONTYPOOL

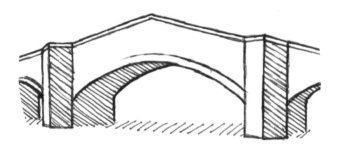

It may or may not have been at the prompting of the Hanbury family of ironmasters that the name Pontypool first appeared on Robert Marden's map of Monmouthshire in 1695. The Hanburys put the town on the map industrially; it was a 'parcel of waste land … with a forge thereon' when Capel Hanbury leased it some thirty years earlier. So possibly they put it on the map quite literally, too.

But my gran always said that it was Pont ap Hywel, really.

You would certainly never have thought that Dafydd ap Hywel was a parson, to look at him, but he was. He was seven foot two in his stockinged feet, broad shouldered, stocky – he was a massive man, fit, healthy and strong as an ox. But he was also very mild-mannered and easy-going. That happens sometimes, of course. It's not always the biggest people or the biggest dogs that are the most inclined to brawls and arguments. He was happy to do a little preaching and a little teaching, he was happy to have a drink and a song – all in all, he lived quite contentedly amongst his parishioners, who were themselves a mixed bunch.

There was really only one nagging little irritation that bothered Dafydd ap Hywel as the years passed by; there was a river – the Afon Llwyd – running cold and brisk between the little settlement and the church on the hill. The path to the church went down into a kind of makeshift fording place, with a few stepping stones slippery with weed. There was no bridge across, and as far as anybody knew there never had been. But a few people had started to think that it was about time there was. And a few more thought that if there was a bridge to be built then Parson Dafydd ap Hywel, wise and mighty, should be the man to build it. And every now and then, his damp-footed congregation would tease him gently, or not so gently, about the unbuilt bridge. Now, over time he began to find this just a little bit wearing. Perhaps, partly because he noticed that although people seemed to think the building of the bridge was his job, none of them ever offered to help him with the task. And so a certain stubbornness settled itself in the parson's mind around the business of the bridge. And the people carried on teasing, and he carried on ignoring them on the outside and feeling a little bit peeved on the inside.

One night, Dafydd ap Hywel had been to see one of his more challenging parishioners – a real 'three-bottle-sinner' with a grudge against everyone and everything. They had sat and talked, and he listened to the man's curses and grumbles long into the night – and to be honest Dafydd had drunk his share from the three bottles too, just to make it more bearable. So around midnight, he was making his way wearily back through the wood, and stumbling a little in the pitch-dark. And he was thinking about the man's parting shot to him as he left the cottage, which wasn't 'Thank you for taking the time to visit me, Parson' or even 'Good night and watch your step on the way home' but 'Catch me in church? Aye, the day you make a bloody bridge to get me there!'

And thinking about that, and feeling pretty gloomy and exasperated – and maybe also just a little bit tipsy – Dafydd said out loud, '*The only bridge people round here will cross is one built by the Devil himself. They'll crowd across that one quick enough!*'

No sooner had he said this than there was a sudden rustle amongst the branches and there, walking beside him through the pitch-dark forest was – another darkness. A Nothing that for a moment nearly froze the blood within him. And the Nothing spoke to Dafydd rather quietly and politely, and said he was very flattered to hear his name called. Doing his best to master his shock, Dafydd told the Devil – now he knew who he was dealing with – that he had *not* called him; he had merely referred to him quite casually, in passing, in a private conversation with himself. But the Devil in the darkness simply smiled and nodded – Dafydd could see his teeth gleaming. He seemed in no hurry to go anywhere and carried on walking companionably beside Dafydd, along the path that wound through the trees. 'Anyway,' said Dafydd ap Hywel stoutly to the Devil, once he had regained full control of his voice, 'it's true enough what I said. Most of the people round here seem keen to go your way. It may as well be you who builds the bridge.'

'Ah!' replied the Devil smoothly and softly. 'Dafydd, Dafydd … don't be in such a hurry to do yourself down! It's true that some few in these parts have been, shall we say, more inclined towards my way of thinking than yours.'

Dafydd snorted. 'Some few! Some few dozen more like.'

'Be that as it may,' the Devil went on, 'that was before you began your ministry. Now it's a different matter entirely. Oh yes indeed, since your arrival I have had my work cut out for me.'

They walked along in silence for a moment, and it has to be said that Dafydd was almost beginning to feel a warm glow of pride at the thought that he really was making a difference for the better in the parish. Then suddenly he remembered who he was talking to and he stopped in his tracks.

'Ha! That's not going to work with me!' said Dafydd. 'You can keep your Devil's flattery! Whatever it is you're after you're not getting it from me so get lost.'

The Devil's lower lip quivered a little at those harsh words.

'How rude!' he said. 'And how ungrateful! You know, I could have bounced up out of nowhere on this moonless night in this dark place and scared the living daylights out of you – or worse. In fact, I'm starting to wish I had. But no, I spoke to you quite politely and truthfully, like any gentleman would.'

And the Devil blew his nose in a big handkerchief, apparently to hide his distress.

Dafydd ap Hywel felt slightly confused. It had been a long night. Perhaps he had spoken a bit roughly. All he really knew was that he was dog-tired, and all his mind could really focus on was his bed. They both stumped on in silence for a while, then the Devil said, 'As a matter of fact, I had been thinking I might offer to lend you a hand with your bridge-building.'

'I am NOT building a bridge!' shouted Dafydd. 'And even if I was, I wouldn't mind betting that there'd be a HELL OF A PRICE to pay for your help.'

'Your choice of words is blunt but fair,' said the Devil with a nod. 'I feel we understand one another.'

Just at that moment they reached the spot where the trees thin away, at the very place in question – the fording point on the Afon Llwyd. Before Dafydd could start splashing his way across, the Devil turned to him and said brightly, 'This has been a most pleasant stroll. But it would be a shame to end our acquaintance so abruptly. I propose a little wager! Let us have a gentleman's understanding and settle this tiresome matter of the bridge once and for all. I propose we go one on each side of the river and pull. And which ever of us gets pulled into the water will be the one who must build the bridge. And whichever of us can pull the other across – well, the bridge will be named in his honour!'

Dafydd hesitated. The sooner this was resolved, he thought to himself, the sooner he could get home to his bed.

'No strings attached? No funny business?'

'Such as?'

'Well … my soul –'

'I'm hurt that you even think it,' said the Devil.

Dafydd cast a still slightly tipsy eye across the river.

'It'll have to be at least thirty by eight, if it's an inch,' he said.

'Yes, yes,' said the Devil impatiently.

Dafydd looked the Devil up and down. There didn't look a lot to him, but he was wiry. Still, Dafydd had a good pair of bellows in his chest – he reckoned he had stamina on his side anyway. It was probably that thought that made him say, a little rashly, 'If we call it best of three, you're on.'

With a whoop of delight the Devil instantly bounded across the stream and stretched out his clawed hands to Dafydd, who braced himself good and hard – but two seconds later there was Dafydd flat on his back in the water, dazed and gasping, too stunned to struggle to his feet. Impatient to clinch the matter, the Devil gave Dafydd a helping hand out of the water, yanking him in to land like a twenty-stone trout. The Devil grinned. He had won the first heat effortlessly. He returned to his side of the river and stretched out his hands again, but this time Dafydd took a moment to steady himself. The cold water had given him the shock he needed and cleared his head. He took a deep breath and took hold of the Devil's outstretched hands, gave a great shout, a clutch and a twist – and this time it was the Devil who went slithering swiftly into the river. In an instant he had bounded out again as if scalded and they stood glaring at one another from opposite banks.

The pair of them sidled up and down a bit, eyeing one another – Dafydd and the Devil both wearing a mask of confidence, but behind the mask both wary, sizing up the other's strength as they got ready for the third, decisive heave. Then with a dodge and a feint they grasped and locked and they began to wrestle.

Then it's arms gripping and feet slipping in the mud and the gravel!

It's pitching and hitching, crashing and splashing and gnashing teeth!

It's the Devil tearing and Dafydd swearing!

And for three hours they wrestle, they kick, they lug and they tug, no seconds, no light in that moonless night and both of them soaking wet for every minute of it.

Until at last, just as he thinks his bellow lungs will burst, Dafydd gives a mighty shuddering heave and the Devil is down, out and

stretched across Dafydd's bank of the river. Dafydd shouts 'Yes!!!'
But before he can say or do anything else the Devil is up and gone
– away into the night, a long, lingering howl floating back through
the trees where he disappeared. And Dafydd keels over, there and
then, on the riverbank, out like a light.

At daybreak, Dafydd wakes. All around him he can see deep
marks in the riverbank where he's dug his heels in and taken the
strain. And when he looks over to the other bank he sees all the
grass is poached up by what looks like the hoofprints of a whole
herd of cattle – or something similar – all facing one way, towards
the river. And there where the final struggle was, the hoofprints
look to be a yard deep in the ground, and there's a young tree with
a scorch mark going three times around the trunk – as if a hot tail
has been wound tightly round it …

And just a few feet away, there in the morning sun, is a sturdy new
bridge of good mortar and stone spanning the river. The Devil had
kept his word and sent his own band of masons in the night. And it
wasn't very long at all before the word got round and people came
from far and wide to see the astonishing bridge. They all came – all
the families of the county. Some people even copied the plan.

> *Herbert and Morgan and Williams, were there*
> *And Kemys and Richards and Van, I swear …*
> *The Monmouthshire folk that have always been here*
> *And always will be till the crack of the sphere*
> *And they all agreed that to hand down the fame*
> *Pont ap Hywel from then would be the best name.*

THE BOAR AND THE SALMON

When Hen Wen the Old White Sow came to shore, with Coll, son of Collfrewy, clinging to her bristled back more dead than alive, she birthed a grain of wheat and a bee, then she rested, heaved herself to her feet and journeyed on, further west and further north. But hers is not the only swine-journey across the land. There are stories of others that came after, across moors and mountains – and in and out of the water, when need compelled; their routes and tracks criss-cross and turn about, here and there. There is one particular boar-hunt that traces a route over land south to Monmouthshire and enters the sea, by a nice symmetry, not so very far from where Hen Wen heaved up onto land. This is the story of the Twrch Trwyth, a king turned by enchantment into a boar, which in turn forms part of the tale of Culhwch and Olwen in the Mabinogi.

A group of Arthur's men are hunting the Twrch Trwyth, not for bacon – perish the thought – but for three items that they have been reliably informed that the Twrch Trwyth has stored between his ears. These three items are a comb, a pair of shears and a razor. They need these things because they are on a quest to fulfil a series of almost impossibly exacting tasks that, if achieved, will win Culhwch son of Cilydd permission to marry Olwen, the daughter of the giant Ysbaddaden Bencawr. The hunt for the Twrch Trwyth is by no means the first of the tasks they have to achieve; in fact, it's one of the last, and before they can even begin the boar hunt they have to find and set free Mabon, who is being held at an unknown location in an impenetrable fortress. A group is selected by Arthur for the mission to find the prison where Mabon is being held. The group includes Cai, Bedwyr, Eiddoel (who is Mabon's cousin) and also the extremely handy Gwrhyr Gwalstawd Ieithoedd. He is of vital importance, because he is Master of Languages and the languages of which he is master include animal and bird speech, and the only way the men can think of to try and find out where Mabon son of Modron might be imprisoned is to ask the oldest and wisest creatures they can find.

So as they travel through Wales, Gwrhyr Gwalstawd Ieithoedd first of all uses his skills to ask directions from the elderly Blackbird of Cilwgwri, who redirects him to the venerable Stag of Rhedynfre, who in turn directs him to the ancient Owl of Cwm Colwyd, then the yet more ancient Eagle of Gwernabwy. And when they ask the

Eagle of Gwernabwy whether he knows anything of the wheareabouts of Mabon son of Modron, who was taken from his mother's bed three nights after his birth, the Eagle says this:

> I came here a long time ago, and when I first came here I rested on a stone, and from its top I would peck the stars every evening. Now the stone is not a handbreadth in height. From that day to this, I have been here, and I have not heard anything of the man of whom you ask. But one time when I was going about seeking my food, over at Llyn Llyw, I struck my claws into a salmon, thinking he could be my food for a long time, but he pulled me into the depths, so that I only just managed to escape from him. Then along with my kindred I launched an attack on him, seeking to destroy him. He, for his part, sent messengers to make peace with me, and he came to me himself to have ten and forty tridents removed from his back. Unless he knows something of the one whom you seek, I know of no one who might know. I, however, will be a guide to you, over to the place where he is.

And the Eagle of Gwernabwy is as good as his word, and he brings the men to a great lake where at last they find the venerable Salmon of Llyn Llyw, the oldest creature in Britain. I wonder if that Salmon is still alive? If he is, he has outlived his home because Llyn Llyw no longer appears on our maps. Where was it, in the days when it was home to the Salmon? Some say that it was a tidal lake in the Severn River itself, or perhaps near the Severn, not far from Caldicot. But others now say that it is the long-lost Monmouth Lake, only recently being retraced by archaeologists yet once a wonder of the world …

When Gwrhyr Gwalstawd Ieithoedd asks his question, the Salmon of Llyn Llyw replies that he does indeed know where Mabon is. He knows because with every flood tide he travels up the Severn (as the bore wave itself does) and so he knows what the Eagle does not know – which is that Mabon son of Modron is being held in prison in Gloucester. Not only that, but to prove that he is telling the truth the Salmon of Llyn Llyw says he will carry

Gwrhyr Gwalstawd Ieithoedd and Cai up river on his shoulders. And he does so. And he was telling the truth.

When Mabon is released, Arthur's men set about fulfilling their remaining tasks and the great boar-chase begins at last. The ferocious Twrch Trwyth leads them on a wild dance around and about the hills and valleys of South Wales until, between Llyn Llyw and the mouth of the Wye there is a confrontation and the Twrch Trwyth, perhaps exhausted by the long overland chase, escapes away into the Severn. And with the strange shaving gear in their possession at last the hunting party head back for a quiet word with Ysbaddaden Bencawr, and a wedding party. Then, with the series of almost-impossible adventures drawn to a close, and the whole assembly fed, watered and pleasantly confused, the stories can begin to be told.

NOTES

1. HEN WEN

The old, old story of Sacred Mother Sow is heard more often now; Cath Little tells it with particular ease and grace. On the Gwent Levels, one of Britain's smallest and rarest bumblebees can still be found. The Shrill Carder bee has been championed by the wonderful Gwent Wildlife Trust and can be found busily pollinating the flowers on the pasturelands of the Levels. So when I tell the story of Hen Wen birthing the first bee on the Levels, I always assume that it was a Shrill Carder.

2. THE STAR-BROWED OX

St Woolos (Gwynllyw's) Cathedral now sits wonderfully atop Stow Hill, Newport. Near Gwladys's bathing place in the Ebbw a covered bath-house once sheltered 'Lady's Well' which may, in fact, have been 'Gwladys Well'. And the hoof prints and bones of the huge aurochs, who made their way through the rich shore-lands like dream-oxen, may still be seen if you know where to look.

3. THE WATERS SALT AND SWEET (1)

The water pumped from the Severn Tunnel during construction would form a lake three miles square and ten yards deep, most of it from the Great Spring.

4. THE WATERS SALT AND SWEET (2)

The Severn is the river that reverses; it flows back on itself in a tidal wave, the second largest on earth. There is a potency around the tides of the Severn Sea and the stories that it carries to the Monmouthshire coast, leaving them like driftwood, scattered and hard to piece together again.

5. HERE I AM

I am, of course, making very free with the imagined thoughts of Julia Somerset (*née* Hamilton), Lady Raglan (1901–1971) in this story. Still, I was encouraged by seeing her photo in the National Portrait Gallery where her gentle, direct gaze doesn't suggest someone who would easily take offence. Her 1939 article in *Folkore* (her only published article) was the first to attach the term 'Green Man' to the familiar architectural feature, the idea having come to her following a visit to St Jerome's.

6. 'UP I GO!'

This tale is found in slightly different versions in various other counties. Storyteller Fiona Eadie does a neat telling of a version from just over the border, involving bonnets instead of sticks. She does some impressive two-handed finger-clicking once the bonnets are tied on, but I'm glad the Monmouthshire version involves a stick because I can only click the fingers on my right hand!

7. Gwarwyn-a-Throt

I've taken my cue from Elisabeth Sheppard-Jones's telling, and she was following John Rhys – but the various tales of Pwca'r Trwyn are some of the most familiar in the region. One strand of the story (not included here) links the Pwca back to a concealed fifteenth-century nobleman and has some strange connections with the building of ap Hywel's bridge.

8. The Prophet

In 1789, at the age of eighty-seven, Edmund Jones preached 405 times. When he visited the local farms he rode his beloved donkey, whose name was Shoned.

9. Tredunnock

Some time after the events of this story, Arthur sent word to Cadoc extending rights of sanctuary in his abode for seven years, seven months and seven days. He also added a dispensation that should any stranger under Cadoc's protection set sail and be driven back by bad weather, they would have leave to return to sanctuary and remain there until the end of their days.

10. The Whitson Henwife

This story, based on one of the tales of the 'Great Flood' of 1607, is a delight to tell. It might have happened in any of the villages along the Levels, but I place it in Whitson.

11. TREACLE

The chapel was dedicated to St Twrog in the sixth century and services were held there for over a thousand years.

12. PEGWS

Pegws was a contemporary of Mary Jones who walked twenty-five miles to Bala to ask Thomas Charles for a Bible. Mary Jones's walk enjoys world-wide fame but the deeds of Pegws are a good deal less well-known.

13. BUTTERCUPS

The church at Llandogo beside the Wye near Tintern is the one and only church dedicated to Euddogwy.

14. *PWLL TRA*

There was indeed a huge landslide in the Nant Carn Valley, long ago. On stormy nights it is said that mournful calls can still be heard from the depths of the reedy pool. I've never been there at night to hear it, though I'm sure the owl has.

15. SPIRIT MARGARET

Mrs Hercules Jenkins' name was Mary. I love this solemn little story.

16. Conjuring at Home

The conjuror's name was Nicholas Johnson. As yet I haven't found out the name of the conjuror's wife.

17. The Secret of the Old Japan House

The secret really was a cause of intense speculation for many years. Towards the end of the nineteenth century, mining expert and naturalist Mr William Adams wrote: *'There is a mineral in the coal-field which has only been worked in the neighbourhood of Pontypool which is there known as the Horn coal, underlying the Meadow Vein coal. It is an oil shale which may be refined ... I have no doubt that Pontypool Japanware obtained its celebrity from the varnish made from this shale.'*

18. Mallt y Nôs

Cŵn Annwn give wild voice – but, much like the Old Woman who calls through the mist, the nearer they are the less their sound is, and the farther away they are the louder they are heard.

19. Black, White and Grey

In her more solid form she is there on the mountains of South East Wales, much as she is on grander mountain ridges in the north of these islands and beyond. Old, massive, her apron full of stones that rolled and tumbled and seamed and gouged the mountainside through ice, and melt, and more ice. Perhaps she's there because the mountains are there, or perhaps it's the other way round.

20. Ten

A similar story is told about the wizard John Charles and The Horse and Jockey at Llanfair Pontymoile.

21. Clean and Clever

The dancing of fairy dances and the hearing of fairy music are a recurrent theme in folk tales and the stories from Gwent are no exception. Thrilling, wistful, strange and familiar, that music and those dances call out for further investigation.

22. Bailey and the Banksman

The 'Crawshay Bailey' song had innumerable verses, with the chorus 'Did you ever see such a funny thing before'. I remember my Gran singing them – doubtless picked up from her uncles, brothers and cousins when she was a girl.

> *Cosher Bailey had an engine*
> *As was always needing mending*
> *And according to her power*
> *She could do four miles an hour.*

> *When she come into the station*
> *She did frighten all the nation*
> *She was wiggle, waggle, wiggle*
> *She was shiggle, shaggle, shiggle.*

She also sang:

> *Well you know my sister Lily*
> *Went to live down in Caerphilly*
> *Cosher Bailey said he'd sack her*

Cos he caught her chewing bacca.

I haven't come across that verse anywhere else yet. Maybe Gran made it up.

23. Red Cloak, Black Hat

The event occurred in October 1772 and 'Mrs Williams miraculous escape from drowning' was a talking point for a long time, with several written accounts also in circulation. The private thoughts of Mrs Williams in my version are based purely on speculation.

24. The Sabbath of the Chair

In later years it is said that those members of the congregation who remembered Morgan Howell considered the Pulpit Chair to be a more precious reminder than the Memorial Chapel in Newport or the grave in Cendl. Their reasoning was that Morgan Howell had no part in making those, but the Chair had been fashioned with his own hands and consecrated with his own words.

25. *Rhamanta!*

Rather than leave Nansi at the bottom of the hill with a lame leg I have opened up the ending of this story to give her a better view, from the hilltop. If you're interested to see a more generally known version of this story, W. Jenkyn Thomas gives a delightful rendering in *The Welsh Fairy Book*. His light touch inspired me in my telling.

26. The Giant

I have taken great liberties with this story. It is usually called 'The Giant of Gilfach Fargoed', famously 'collected' by the boys of Lewis School as an example of local oral tradition. It can now be found in a variety of forms; I add my telling here as a somewhat altered perspective on the theme.

27. Rich Man, Poor Man, Beggar Man, Thief

It is debatable whether any of the four titles accurately fitted the historical William Jones and the whole story has been called a load of twaddle (or similar). But there's no doubt that he endowed the Haberdasher's School in Monmouth. Besides which, Joe King is an inspiration regardless of whether he actually existed or not.

28. Pontypool

There's clearly history to the clergy/bridge-building debate. The parish records of Panteg for 1754 note 'A new Arch bridge erected at Pontymoile where never was one before by order of Mr Hanbury or his Clerk, but charged to ye parish of Panteague. Ye Rector of Panteague has not paid towards it.' Someone, possibly ye Rector himself, has crossed out the last few words very firmly and written in their place '*is not obliged* to pay towards it.'

29. The Boar and the Salmon

The Twrch Trwyth's progress through Wales forms part of the story of Culhwch and Olwen, which we find in the Mabinogion; it comes to us via the White Book of Rhydderch, the Red Book of Hergest and the musings of many dreamers. If it seems strange that the Eagle of Gwernabwy does not know where Mabon is being held, Lee Raye suggests on his *historyandnature* site that it might be because he was a white-tailed eagle, familiar in southern Britain at the time of this tale. A white-tailed eagle would hunt salmon near the coast, but not all the way inland to Gloucester.

BIBLIOGRAPHY

BOOKS

Barber, Chris, *Arthurian Caerleon in Literature and Legend* (Blorenge Books: Abergavenny, 1996)

—, *Eastern Valley: The Story of Torfaen* (Blorenge Books: Abergavenny, 1999)

—, *Hando's Gwent* (Blorenge Books: Abergavenny, 2000)

—, *Mysterious Wales* (David & Charles: Newton Abbott, 1982)

—, *More Mysterious Wales* (David & Charles: Newton Abbott, 1986)

Barber, Chris and Pykitt, David, *Journey to Avalon* (Blorenge Books: Abergavenny, 1993)

Baring-Gould, S. and Fisher, John, *The Lives of the British Saints (in four volumes)* (The Honorable Society of Cymmrodorion: London, 1907–11)

Bielski, Alison, *Flower Legends of the Wye Valley* (Chepstow, 1974)

Briggs, Katherine, *A Dictionary of Fairies* (Allen Lane: London, 1976)

Bromwich, Rachel, *Trioedd Ynys Prydein* (University of Wales Press, revised edition, 2006)

C.H.W. *The legends of Gwent* (W.M. Christophers: Newport, 1857)

Clarke, Stephen, *The Lost Lake*, revised edition (Monmouth Archaeological Society, 2016)

Coxe, William, *An Historical Tour through Monmouthshire* (1801)

Davies, Geraint Eurig (ed.), *Border Voices – Poems of Gwent and Monmouthshire* (Gwasg Gomer: Llandysul, 1999)

Davies, L. Twiston, *Men of Monmouthshire* (*Western Mail and Echo*: Cardiff, 1933)

Davies W.H., *The Complete Poems* (Jonathan Cape: London, 1963)

Edmonds, Joyce (ed.), *Tales of the People of Old St. Arvans* (Village Books: Chepstow, 1990)

Gwent Federation of Women's Institutes, The, *The Gwent Village Book* (1994)

Gwent, Theatr (ed.), *Footprints Stuck Forever* (Theatr Gwent, 2000)

Hando, Fred J., *Journeys in Gwent* (Newport, 1951)

—, *Monmouthshire Sketch Book* (Newport, 1954, reprint 1958)

—, *The Pleasant Land of Gwent* (Newport, 1944, reprint 1958)

Howell, Raymond, *Searching for the Silures* (The History Press: Stroud, 2006)

Hughes, Kristoffer, *The Book of Celtic Magic* (Llywelyn: US, 2014)

John, W.D. and Simcox, Anne, *Pontypool and Usk Japanned Wares* (Harding & Curtis: Bath, 1966)

Jones, Edmund, *A Geographical, Historical and Religious Account of the Parish of Aberystruth* (Treveca 1779, reprint J.E. Owen 1988)

—, *A Relation of the Apparition of Spirits in the County of Monmouth and the Principality of Wales* (Treveca 1780, reprint Newport, 1813)

Jones, Francis, *The Holy Wells of Wales* (University of Wales Press: Cardiff, 1954, reprint 1998)

Kissack, Keith, *The River Severn* (Dalton: Lavenham,1982)

Lloyd, W.G., *Tales of Torfaen* (Tonypandy, 2000)

Michael, D.P.M., *The Mapping of Monmouthshire* (Regional Publications, 1985)

Nichols, Reginald, *Pontypool and Usk Japan Ware* (Pontypool, 1981)

Olding, Frank, *Folklore of Blaenau Gwent* (Blaenau Gwent County Borough Council, 1995)

—, *The Archaeology of Upland Gwent* (Royal Commission on the Ancient and Historical Monuments of Wales, 2016)

Palmer, Roy, *The Folklore of (old) Monmouthshire* (Logaston Press: Almeley, 1998)

Phillips, Edgar (Trefin), *Edmund Jones 'The Old Prophet'* (1959)

Rees, W.J. (ed.), *Lives of the Cambro-British Saints* (Llandovery, 1853)

Rhys, John, *Celtic Folklore: Welsh and Manx* (Oxford University Press, 1901)

Roderick, Alan, *Haunted Gwent* (Handpost: Newport, 1995)

—, *The Folklore of Gwent* (Village Publishing, 1983)

Sheppard-Jones, Elisabeth, *Stories of Wales* (John Jones: Cardiff, 1976)

Sikes, Wirt, *British Goblins: Welsh Foklore, Fairy Mythology, Legends and Traditions* (Sampson Low: London, 1880)

—, *Rambles and Studies in South Wales* (Sampson Low: London, 1881)

Stephen, D. Rhys, *Pwka'r Trwyn, The Celebrated Mynyddislwyn Sprite* (Prize essay at the Newport Eisteddfod, London 1851)

Thomas, Keith, *Heritage: A History of Ebbw Vale Volume 1* (Kerin: Pontnewydd, 2000)

Thomas, W. Jenkyn, *The Welsh Fairy Book* (A&C Black: London, 1938)

Trevelyan, Marie, *Folk-lore and Folk-stories of Wales* (Elliot Stock: London, 1909)

Walker, Thomas A., *The Severn Tunnel* (Kingsmead Reprints, 1990)

Newspapers

The Pontypool Free Press
The South Wales Argus
The Monmouthshire Merlin .
The Usk Gleaner and Monmouthshire Record

PERIODICALS

Davies, T.A., 'Folk-lore of Gwent: Monmouthshire legends and traditions', *Folklore*, 48 (1937)

Morris, Abraham, 'Morgan Howell's Pulpit Chair at Rock Chapel, Blackwood' *Cylchgrawn Cymdeithas Hanes y Methodistiaid Calfinaidd*, 4–6 (1918–21), pp. 71–75

Raglan, Lady, 'The Green Man in Church Architecture', *Folklore*, 50 (1939), pp. 45–57

Wherry, Beatrix A., 'Wizardry on the Welsh Border', *Folklore*, 15 (1904), pp. 75–86

'Miscellaneous Notes from Monmouthshire', *Folklore*, 16 (1905), pp. 63–7

WEBSITES

greenmanenigma.com
maryinmonmouth.blogspot.com
whitedragon.org.uk/articles/Sabrina
wondersofbritain.org
twmbarlwm.co.uk
historyandnature.wordpress.com

Society *for* Storytelling

Since 1993, The Society for Storytelling has championed the ancient art of oral storytelling and its long and honourable history – not just as entertainment, but also in education, health, and inspiring and changing lives. Storytellers, enthusiasts and academics support and are supported by this registered charity to ensure the art is nurtured and developed throughout the UK.

Many activities of the Society are available to all, such as locating storytellers on the Society website, taking part in our annual National Storytelling Week at the start of every February, purchasing our quarterly magazine Storylines, or attending our Annual Gathering – a chance to revel in engaging performances, inspiring workshops, and the company of like-minded people.

You can also become a member of the Society to support the work we do. In return, you receive free access to Storylines, discounted tickets to the Annual Gathering and other storytelling events, the opportunity to join our mentorship scheme for new storytellers, and more. Among our great deals for members is a 30% discount off titles from The History Press.

For more information, including how to join, please visit

www.sfs.org.uk